Also by LARI DON

Spellchasers

The Witch's Guide to Magical Combat

LARI DON

Kelpies

Kelpies is an imprint of Floris Books
First published in 2017 by Floris Books
© 2017 Lari Don

The publisher acknowledges subsidy from
Creative Scotland towards the publication
of this volume

 Also available as an eBook

British Library CIP Data available
ISBN 978-178250-307-1
Printed in Poland

For Gowan

Thank you for the riddles, party games and
bike helmets, and for asking awkward questions,
insisting on the final scene and throwing socks.
I really couldn't do this without you

Chapter One

When Molly heard her neighbours' cat miaow, she shrank instantly, feeling the familiar flash of heat through her bones.

But when she ran from the noise of the cat, she felt an unfamiliar weight whipping around behind her. Did she have a long tail?

She didn't have time to worry about what animal she'd shifted into, because she realised she wasn't running fast enough to get away from a cat. She wasn't leaping and sprinting, she was scuttling and dashing.

Why was she moving so slowly, so weakly?

She glanced round. Yes, she did have a tail. A long thin brown tail. The skinny length meant she was probably a rodent, the brown hair meant she definitely wasn't a rat.

But her glance back had shown her something even more worrying than her new shape.

Poppet, the fluffy white cat from next door, was stalking her. Belly low, paws stretching forward, eyes fixed on Molly's ridiculous tail.

Molly had a choice.

She could run to one of the gaps in the garden fence, because fences and walls normally shifted her back to her girl form. But that might not work this time, because the rules of her own personal magic seemed to have altered today.

Or she could hide from the cat now and shift back later, when she wasn't in immediate danger.

Her scared body decided for her. She desperately wanted to hide. So she darted towards the hole she could see under the shed. The hole was tiny, but as a mouse or a vole or a shrew or whatever she was, she might fit inside.

She ran as fast as she could, on these spindly short legs, with that nonsensical tail and this light body too close to the ground, feeling exposed and vulnerable on the flat winter grass of her own back garden.

Suddenly she was aware of the heat and speed of the cat behind her. She felt the air move round her tail as Poppet pounced.

Molly veered to her left and the cat's shadow passed over her. The cat's body crashed down onto the patch of grass Molly had been scurrying across a fraction of a second before.

Poppet whirled round, trying to work out where her prey had gone, and Molly kept running.

She'd learnt two ways to run in the last four months. Full speed ahead in a straight line, to beat her friend Innes in shapeshifter races. And tricksy leaping and dodging, to evade predators.

So she didn't run straight towards the shed. Even with the smaller body, weaker legs and lesser speed of a tiny rodent, she moved like a hare across the grass: running fast, slowing down, leaping left, dodging right, constantly changing speed and direction.

It wasn't likely that Poppet had ever met a mouse who moved so unpredictably, and Molly kept just ahead of the cat's claws.

She reached the hole and dived in. She slid right to the back, snug and safe in the cramped dark.

Molly Drummond was used to suddenly becoming small and fast. But suddenly becoming small and *slow*, that was new and scary.

The noise of a cat had never triggered her curse before. She'd never become a long-tailed rodent either. Normally dog noises triggered the curse; normally she became a hare. But nothing was normal today.

Poppet's paw prodded at the entrance to the hole. Her hot fishy biscuity breath filled the space. However, the cat was too big to get in and Molly was too far back to be dragged out.

As she crouched there, panting and shivering, she wondered what had just happened.

Molly had been cursed by an angry witch last autumn, so that she turned into a hare – like a bigger stronger

9

faster rabbit – whenever she heard a dog bark or growl. And she stayed a hare until she crossed a boundary, usually the boundary between gardens or farms.

She'd learnt to control the curse, so she could shift into a hare whenever she wanted to, for speed or size or even for fun. But she still had to cross a boundary to become a girl again, so she was now an expert on land boundaries in her own Edinburgh neighbourhood, and boundaries round the town of Craigvenie, further north, where she'd been cursed.

Apart from a few days last year when the witch had altered the curse so it was harder to shift back, Molly's curse had been stable and manageable for months. Until today.

So she'd better go north, to see if the friends whose curses she'd lifted last year could help her work out why her curse had become more dangerous. But she couldn't go to Speyside until she got out from under this shed and became a girl again.

Molly shivered as she watched Poppet's paw withdraw at last. She crouched in the dark, wondering how she would cope if she was stuck as this trembling and terrified creature forever. Because if the rules or strength of her curse had somehow changed, perhaps crossing a boundary wouldn't shift her back?

There was only one way to find out. She moved to the entrance of the hole, her whiskers snuffling and jerking. She couldn't smell cat breath. She couldn't sense animal heat or hear a huge heartbeat.

Poppet had probably given up. It was probably safe.

Molly hesitated. She didn't want to leave the security of this dusty dark hole. But she gathered all the courage she could find in her tiny shaking body, dashed out of the hole and ran towards the nearest gap in the fence.

A white shape leapt from the shed roof, bounded onto the top of the fence and landed on the grass, paw slashing down to trap the tiny form on the ground.

And Poppet scratched the knuckle of Molly's human thumb.

The cat backed off, white fur standing up along her spine.

Molly smiled. "Sorry to give you a fright, Poppet."

She climbed over the wooden fence and ran to her back door, hoping the cat wouldn't miaow again before she got inside.

She rushed into the living room. "Mum, Dad, can I go to Aunt Doreen's next week, for the February holidays?"

Her mum said, "Again? You stayed with Doreen last tattie holidays and complained the whole way up the A9. But then you pestered us to take you up at Christmas, and now you want to go again next week? What's in Speyside that you can't get in Edinburgh?"

"My friends in Craigvenie," said Molly. But she was also thinking about the magic she'd discovered up north, which made Craigvenie the best place to find out why her curse had suddenly become so much stranger and more dangerous.

She looked at her dad. "When I'm with my Craigvenie friends, we play in the woods, by the rivers and in the hills, like you did when you were wee."

He smiled. "It's a good place to grow up. If the snow holds off, I'll drive you north."

So Molly went upstairs to pack, and to work out how to avoid cats as well as dogs for the next three days.

Chapter Two

Molly said hi to her Aunt Doreen and bye to her dad, who was having a scone before driving home, then she threw her bag into the tiny sloped-ceiling spare room and dashed back outside to lift her bike from the boot of the car.

She cycled through Craigvenie and ran through the woods to her best friend Beth's house. Beth's Aunt Jean said, "She's gone up into the hills with Innes and Atacama. Something about talking to a statue? They've just left; you might catch them."

Molly knew there was only one statue that Innes had conversations with, so she cycled fast on the road leading towards the snow-topped mountains in the distance, then more slowly over the moorland path to the river where the statue was hidden.

Innes must have been heading towards the hills reluctantly, because if he'd galloped enthusiastically the whole way, she'd never have caught up. But eventually she saw her friends ahead of her. Beth, the dryad, with her black clothes and purple hair, her silver jewellery glinting in the cold sunlight. Innes, the kelpie, in his blond-haired jeans-wearing boy form, rather than his white-maned horse form. And Atacama, the sphinx, looking like a puma-sized black cat, apart from the small wings on his back and his long almost-human face.

"Hey!" Molly yelled. "Wait for me!"

They all stopped and waved cheerfully at her, as she wobbled along the bumpy path.

When she reached them, she jumped off her bike and asked Innes, "Why are you still coming up here? He's not going to get any politer."

"I only come up once a month now. You're right, he's still wasting the five minutes he's free from the stone calling me names, rather than promising he won't eat our neighbours. But I have to try."

"Have you told your mum yet?"

"Have I told my mother that I cursed my father? You've got to be kidding! She thinks he's on a long hunting expedition."

"Four months long?" Molly laid her bike on the heather.

Innes shrugged. "She thinks he's hunting far from home, when he's actually stuck as a statue because he kept hunting too close to home."

Beth hugged Molly. "We didn't think you were coming back until Easter."

"I need your help, because my curse has gone weird. Come over to this burn and I'll show you. It's a boundary, isn't it?"

They all nodded.

Molly stood on the edge of the narrow burn. "Atacama, make a noise like a pet cat."

"Don't be so insulting."

"Just as an experiment. Please."

He purred, lighter and softer than his normal big cat rattle.

Molly became a mouse, jumped into the shockingly cold water, paddled across and pulled herself out on the other side, as a girl.

She turned round. Beth looked worried, Innes was frowning and Atacama had his usual stony calm face.

Molly said, "Now, Beth, hoot like an owl."

Beth made a long eerie noise, like the owls that swooped through her birch trees at night.

Molly shifted into another tiny rodent, with less tail. She wondered if she was a vole, as she swam back across the burn.

"It's not just rodents," she said, after she'd shifted to a girl again. "Can you do a smaller bird, Beth, a thrush or something?"

Beth sang a quick trill of notes.

And Molly became something she'd never been before. Something legless and spineless. She felt fingers pick her up and carry her over the boundary, then she fell to the ground.

"A worm?" snapped Beth. "Really? You wanted me to turn you into a worm?"

Molly shook her head. "I expected to become a snail:

that's what happened when I heard birdsong in the garden on Thursday. Anyway, this is how my curse has gone weird. Whatever predator I hear, I become its prey. Mousey things, creepy crawlies, all sorts of little edible creatures. It's risky being too far from a boundary, because I can't sprint as most of these animals. Though it could be fun too. Can anyone do a convincing wolf?"

Innes raised his face to the sky and howled.

Molly became a slim long-legged deer.

Before she crossed the water, she turned away from her friends and bounded across the heather, to enjoy the speed, the smells, the drumming of hooves on the ground. Then she turned back and leapt the burn, landing and jumping up as a girl.

Innes laughed.

Molly grinned. "It's only the hare I can choose to become. I think all the other animals have to be triggered by a noise outside me. But I haven't experimented yet. It's too dangerous on my own."

"Molly, that's horrible," said Beth.

Innes said, "It's not horrible. It's amazing! You can shapeshift into lots more animals than I can. Most of which I'm going to thrash in a race. A horse against a mouse or a worm, that's going to be so easy. I'm going to win everything this holiday!"

"No more races!" said Beth. "You can't stay like this, Molly. You have to get rid of this curse. You surely don't want to be a worm ever again?"

"I didn't want to be a worm that time."

Beth frowned. "This wouldn't have happened if you'd ever truly committed to doing whatever is necessary to lift your curse."

"That's hardly fair, Beth! I've done magical homework, fought hungry monsters and defeated a warrior queen. I've even been polite to the witch who cursed me. I'm not sure how much more committed I could be to lifting my curse. Anyway, what do you mean by 'whatever is necessary'? Do you mean becoming a witch? You know the only way I can force Mr Crottel to lift the curse is to beat him in magical combat, and the only way I can do that is to embrace my ancestors' heritage and become a witch. But given the choice between being a part-time hare or a full-time witch, both of which you object to because you say all dark magic is bad, I still think the cursed hare is a better option."

"Which is handy for you, because you like being a hare," said Beth.

"Yes, I do." She smiled at Beth. "I know it's inconvenient and dangerous, but if I hadn't been cursed I wouldn't have met all of you. Also, I get to beat Innes in races."

Innes grinned. "You don't always beat me, sometimes we cross the finish line together."

"That's only happened once. You've never actually won. So, I'm good at being a hare and I enjoy it, most of the time. But I feel really vulnerable as a tiny rodent, and when I'm not a mammal I feel like I might forget about my real self and forget to cross a boundary. That's why I got Dad to drive me up here: to find out why my curse has started turning me into other prey animals, and to stop it. Maybe Beth is right, and I should try one more time to get rid of the original curse."

Innes said, "When you helped us lift our curses, we promised to help you lift yours. So if you're sure this is what you want...?"

Molly nodded at him.

"...then I will help you break your curse."

"Me too," said Atacama.

"And me," said Beth. "But surely you don't want to become a witch?"

"Of course not. So we'd better find another way to stop me becoming a mouse or a worm."

Innes looked up at the sky. "It's almost noon."

As they walked towards the pool where Innes's father lay, Atacama asked Molly, "Did you annoy another witch? Someone who cast a more powerful curse or somehow enhanced Mr Crottel's curse?"

"I don't think so."

Beth said, "Do you think Mr Crottel made the curse stronger himself? He threatened to make it worse again if we kept nagging him to lift it, but you haven't spoken to him since October."

Molly shrugged. "I suppose we could visit Mrs Sharpe, see how big the Promise Keeper is now and look at my curse mirror. It might show what's happened."

Atacama said, "Or we could ask Theo to use his family's library of scrolls, to research what magic might enhance a curse."

"Or we could simply speak to Mr Crottel, find out what's he's done and persuade him to lift the whole curse," said Beth.

"First, I need to speak to my dad," said Innes, as they reached the river. "Back off, everyone. I don't want him blaming you."

Molly, Beth and Atacama sat down in the heather a dozen paces away.

"Why hasn't he told his mum?" whispered Molly.

Beth whispered back, "I think he's scared to..."

Atacama nodded. "He's convinced he can sort it out himself. But she's starting to ask awkward questions."

"Innes cursed his dad and he's lying to his mum," said Beth. "All that dark magic and deception must be damaging him. Now that you've agreed your curse is a bad thing, Molly, you can help persuade Innes to lift this curse too. Then we can all be free of dark magic, before we even move up to secondary school!"

Molly sighed. She wasn't sure she had agreed that her curse was all bad. She wouldn't miss being a mouse, but she would miss being a hare. And Innes had a good reason for cursing his dad.

She looked over at Innes, standing at the edge of a large rock above a deep pool in the river. Then she glanced up at the sun, gleaming silver through the grey clouds. As far as she could tell, it was now noon. Innes's dad was released from the curse at noon, for five minutes, every five days.

Molly noticed a dark winged shape in the sky. She flinched, thinking it was a crow. But it was higher up, moving in a lazy circle, like a bird of prey. So long as she didn't hear it make a sound, the bird wasn't a danger to her.

She looked back at Innes, still alone on the rock.

Innes checked the position of the sun, glanced into the pool, then turned to his friends and shrugged. He knelt down and stared into the clear water moving beneath him.

"I can see him," Innes called. "But why isn't he…?" Innes dived into the water, shifting on the way into a long silver-and-green stripy fish.

Beth yelled, "No! His dad might be trying to lure him in!"

Atacama leapt up and ran towards the rock. "He could ambush Innes and break the curse by defeating him in combat!"

Molly and Beth followed. They all looked down and saw the long sharp-nosed pike prodding at a horse lying at the bottom of the pool.

The horse was jerking, kicking feebly at Innes's fish form.

"If that's an ambush," said Atacama, "it's not a very effective one."

The horse shifted into a man curled on the riverbed. The man moved his arms weakly, then he changed into a pike too, which wriggled off the pebbles and started to rise to the surface, belly-up.

Suddenly the fish turned to grey stone and sank to the bottom again.

Now there were two fish visible in the pool. One shining bright as it swam through the water, the other flat and grey on the bottom, like the swimming pike's dull heavy shadow. The silvery pike circled the stone pike, nosing and nudging.

Past the ripples in the clear water, Molly could see cracks in the stone fish.

Innes rose out of the river. He changed to a boy as he broke the surface, then scrambled up the rock.

"Something's going horribly wrong!" he gasped. "My dad is ill or injured or something. Did you see? He couldn't move properly. He couldn't jump out as a horse, or climb out as a man, or swim properly as a fish. And when he turned back to stone, like I'd cursed him to do, the stone was all fractured and crumbling!" He rubbed his hands over his face. "I must have done something wrong when I cast the curse. Now the rock is breaking and it's damaging him. He's dying. I'm killing him!"

Chapter Three

"Your dad is still alive." Molly put her hand on Innes's shoulder. "We all saw him moving."

"But how long will he stay alive? How long has this been happening?" Innes looked anxiously at the water. "I was up here in January and he was fine then. Well, not *fine*: he was angry, but he was healthy. What have I done? What can I do?"

Beth said, "There's only one thing you can do. Lift the curse, now."

"Of course. Beth's answer to everything. 'Dark magic is bad. Just say no. Lift the curse.' But it's not that simple. He was *eating fairies*, Beth. He was hunting hikers. He's a monster. I trapped him in the stone to protect my neighbours, which includes you and your family. If I lift the curse without the promise that he won't hunt near our rivers, we're all at risk."

"Especially you," said Atacama quietly.

"Yes. Especially me. He keeps saying he'll take his revenge as soon as he's free. If I lift the curse without a promise he won't hunt near home, I'll be his next prey."

He stared at the grey stone fish in the water. "If I don't lift it, he'll fall apart. He'll die. There must be other ways to stop his irresponsible hunting. Though I can't think of any, which is why I cast the curse in the first place. But I have to lift the curse soon." He sighed. "I have to lift it now."

"We'll make sure you don't suffer for doing the right thing," said Beth. "We'll protect you."

Innes laughed. "My father is a predator, a carnivore, a hunter. Beth, your personal superpower is talking to trees, Atacama is great at riddles, and Molly can become lots of small, easily squashed creatures. I appreciate your offer of protection, but he could rip you apart on his way to me. Don't protect me. Protect yourselves. So promise me, if he attacks, you won't interfere?"

"No, I won't promise that," said Molly. "Don't be daft, Innes. I'm not going to leave you to face him on your own."

"Me neither," said Atacama. "I may be the riddle master, but I also have teeth and claws."

"We're a team," said Beth. "When you lift this curse, we'll be standing right beside you."

Innes stared at them all. "I suppose I wouldn't make a promise like that either." He nodded. "Right, let's do this."

He stood on the very edge of the rock and spoke clearly: "I, Innes Milne, wish to lift the curse I cast on my father, Fraser Milne, kelpie of the Spey valley. I free him from the rock. I lift the curse."

He raised his hands. The water trembled.

But the fish was still flat on the bottom of the pool.

Then the fish twitched.

Out of the corner of her eye, Molly saw the circling black bird fall from the sky.

It didn't fall to earth in a controlled dive to catch prey, but in a tumbling wingless plummet. Molly wondered if the bird had died the moment Innes lifted the curse. She wondered if the bird was a curse-hatched.

Molly heard a splash, so she stopped searching the horizon for the fallen bird and looked at the river.

Innes had dived into the pool in human form and was trying to drag his father out.

At first he was trying to lift a motionless man off the riverbed. Then the man started to grow tentacles and fangs, and Innes swam rapidly backwards. Then the half-formed monster squidged into a large fish. Innes grabbed the pike and swam to the edge of the pool.

Innes yelled in frustration when the fish turned into a horse and slipped back under.

He was struggling to haul the horse out of the water, so his friends jumped off the rock onto the riverbank to help. Molly and Beth pulled, Innes and Atacama shoved, and the horse dug his hooves into the riverbed and pushed. Eventually, the grey stallion lay on the bank, breath rattling, ribcage heaving, splits in his dappled skin leaking blood.

He kicked out at Innes with a front hoof.

"Back off," Innes yelled at his friends. "He's dangerous!"

But the horse was lying still now, his legs limp on the ground.

Then the horse shifted into a man.

A long-limbed heavy-shouldered man, with shaggy greying hair. He had rips in his shirt and trousers, and wounds in the skin underneath. The man glared at them, from one eye black with bruising and one eye oozing yellow pus.

He sat up slowly.

Innes stepped forward to help.

"Don't touch me!" the man croaked. "Don't touch me, you curse-casting coward." He held up his hands, wincing as he tried to straighten fingers that were bent at odd angles. "That rock you've trapped me inside is crumbling, and I'm falling apart too. I can feel every crack, every chip breaking off. It's agony. Your curse is torturing me, Innes." He coughed. "I will make you pay for that pain!"

He stood up and lurched towards his son. Molly, Atacama and Beth moved closer, to protect Innes if his father attacked. But Mr Milne stumbled and bent over, spluttering and spitting frothy blood onto the heather.

"The curse is gone," said Innes, softly. "I've just lifted it."

His father looked up. "Do you want me to thank you? You're the one who made me suffer all those months.

I'll thank you properly once I have my strength back."

Mr Milne leant against the rock and ran his fingers through his thick grey hair. "How will I thank you? I might lame you as a horse, so you can't run. I might rot your teeth as a pike, so you can't eat. I've been dreaming up nightmare curses for you, my darling son."

He stood up straight, grunting with the effort. "I don't want your mother to see me like this, or to talk me out of my rightful revenge. So before I go home, I'll find someone to heal these wounds, then I'll hunt for you…"

Innes's father limped away.

"Dad, please, let me explain." Innes started to follow.

Beth held him back. "He's too angry. Leave him alone just now."

They watched the injured kelpie struggle across the moorland. Away from Craigvenie, away from his home. Away from his rivers.

Innes sighed.

Molly said, "I think I saw a curse-hatched fall over there, when you lifted the curse. But it didn't look like a crow. Let's go and check."

"Why bother?" said Innes. "I don't care if it was a crow or a sparrow or a parrot or a pterodactyl. I've lifted the curse, but my dad's still wounded and still wants revenge… I don't want to see the corpse of a bird I just killed."

Atacama said, "But if the curse-hatched for your curse isn't a crow, that's odd. It's worth investigating."

He bounded off, sniffing and searching the heather, as Beth and Molly ran after him. Innes trudged behind.

"Here!" The sphinx stood with his head down, his ears pricked, his tail flicking.

Molly saw the crumpled body of a huge black bird with a vicious hooked beak. When it was flying, she'd thought it was a hawk, or maybe a kite. But this was...

"An eagle?" said Beth. "A curse-hatched eagle? It can't be."

Atacama grabbed the tip of the bird's right wing in his jaws, and pulled it gently, to straighten it out.

On the wing, Molly could see the image of a stone in a river, the breeze on the feathers rippling the water against the rock.

Atacama dropped the wing. "It's definitely a curse-hatched."

"But curse-hatched are crows," said Beth. "Always and only ever crows. A crow hatches from a stone egg every time a curse is cast. That crow grows strong on the power of its curse. If the curse is strong enough and lasts long enough, the curse-hatched can shift between crow and human, like Corbie. Then the crow dies when the curse is broken or lifted. That's what a curse-hatched *is*, a *crow* hatched from a stone egg by a curse. Not an eagle."

"Yet here it is, in front of us," said Atacama. "If Corbie wants to continue his mother's dream of creating an army, birds of prey might be better curse-hatched soldiers for him."

"What curse-hatched soldiers?" asked Innes, walking slowly towards them.

Atacama lifted the black eagle by its neck and dragged it to Innes's feet.

Innes stared at the image on the wing. "This is a curse-hatched? I hatched this eagle, with the curse I cast on my father? How? I'm not a strong magic-user. It was just a spur of the moment spell, to stop him chasing and eating our neighbours. How could I do this? And how could I get the curse so wrong that it was wounding him?"

"He was fine last month, wasn't he?" asked Molly.

Innes nodded.

"Then this is new. His curse becoming stronger and more damaging, and a curse-hatched bird that's an eagle rather than a crow. Maybe it's all connected."

Beth said, "Your curse has also just become stronger and more damaging, Molly. I wonder what your curse-hatched looks like now?"

Molly thought of the soft baby bird she'd held last year, with the image of a hare on its wing. Then she looked at the hooked beak of the curse-hatched eagle at her feet. "We need more information before we can work out what's going on."

Beth nodded. "So let's go and ask Mr Crottel what's happened to the curse he cast on you."

"He might not know," said Innes. "I've no idea what happened to the curse I cast on my dad."

Molly sighed. "Beth's probably right. My curse-caster

has made changes to my curse before, so it makes sense to start by asking him."

As she turned to head back to Craigvenie, Molly glanced up and saw another large bird of prey, soaring in the air currents above. Then she heard a high yelping cry.

And she fell over.

She struggled up onto tiny fragile feet, balanced on long wobbly legs and looked with unfocussed eyes at the shadowy shape above her.

The black shape became larger and larger, swooping down towards her.

Molly stumbled on her pathetic legs towards Beth, who was waving her arms at the bird and shouting, "Shoo!"

The eagle yelped again and soared towards the thin clouds.

Beth picked Molly up. "This constant shapeshifting into unlikely animals could be very inconvenient. But you are nice and cuddly this time." She carried Molly towards the narrow burn.

Molly looked at her bony white legs and realised what she was. She nuzzled at Beth's arm.

"Ok!" said Beth. "If you're sure."

Molly leapt down and walked through the heather, lifting her little hooves high. She started to bounce and jump. Not sideways or forwards like she did as a hare, but up and down, on the spot, just for fun.

Then she danced and bounced all the way to the burn, leapt over it and landed on the other side as a girl.

"Was I a lamb? Was that eagle trying to eat me as a lamb?"

"Yes, you were a lamb. No, it probably wasn't trying to eat you." Innes jumped over to join her. "If that was your curse-hatched, it needs you to stay alive so it can live on the energy of your curse. And if it wasn't your curse-hatched, we would have protected you. So you weren't in any danger. But you *were* fluffy and cute." He grinned. "A little frolicking lamb, like the first sign of spring!"

"I'm glad I've cheered you up."

"Were you deliberately frolicking? With your curse mutating, and my dad swearing revenge on me, did you actually take time out to frolic?"

"I couldn't help it!" said Molly. "With those spindly legs and this tall heather, it was the only possible way to move."

Innes raised his eyebrows.

"Ok. You're right. But I was a *lamb*. I had to frolic a little bit!"

Beth jumped the burn too. "Right, off we go to Mr Crottel's. And if you're *really* polite when you ask about your curse, he might even decide you've suffered enough and lift it completely!" She strode cheerfully towards Craigvenie.

As they followed, Molly said to Innes and Atacama, "Just as well I took that chance to frolic. Because if Mr Crottel lifts my curse today, that might be the last time I ever change shape..."

Chapter Four

Molly skirted the constantly renewed piles of dog dirt that had led to her discovering the world of magic and curses last year. She'd shouted at Mr Crottel for throwing his dogs' mess onto the pavement, and he'd responded by putting a curse on her so she turned into a hare every time she heard a dog.

Molly opened Mr Crottel's rusty gate and walked up the garden path, past a pile of mouldering sofa cushions, a box of rusty dog food tins, and a line of outdoor lights stuck in the lumpy lawn. She saw his two dogs looking out of the grimy living-room window. At least if they were inside they couldn't chase her.

She glanced over her shoulder to check her friends were visible at the gate, then knocked on the door.

Mr Crottel opened the door dressed in his stained greeny-grey suit, scratching his stubbly jaw. "Hare-girl! Are you still alive? Your spine hasn't been snapped by a fast hound yet? What a shame! What do you want this time?"

"I want to know what you've done to my curse."

"I haven't done anything to your curse. And I'm not going to. Lifting a curse would damage my reputation as a dark-magic user. So I'm never going to lift it, however much you beg!"

"I'm not begging, I'm just asking."

"Why?" He scratched his armpit. "Why are you asking now? What's happened to your curse?" He leant out of the doorway, his drooping face uncomfortably close to Molly. "I have a right to know. It's my curse. You're my curse victim. Tell me!"

Molly shook her head. "If you didn't change it yourself, you don't need to know."

He grinned. "You don't like it, whatever it is!" Then he frowned. "But I don't want someone else interfering in my curse. And now you're back on my territory, I don't want someone else ending your punishment by eating you. If anyone is going to end your curse like that, it will be me. So if you won't tell me what's going on, I'll trigger your curse, right now!"

Mr Crottel waved his hand and the gate slammed shut behind Molly. He stepped onto the path and the front door slammed shut behind him.

Then Mr Crottel shifted.

Not fast like Molly shifted, nor smooth like Innes shifted.

Mr Crottel shook himself apart.

He shook himself like an animal shaking itself dry. As he shook, his suit flew off him in ragged strips. So did his skin. The strips of flesh and fabric whirled around him in a blur, obscuring his shape, then reattached themselves, forming fur and ears and paws.

Mr Crottel became a huge dog.

A huge green dog.

His hair was shaggy and matted, the colour of new snot or old bruises. His eyes burnt like gassy blue flames. His stringy drool was eggy yellow. He smelt worse than the dog dirt on the pavement.

And he was massive.

He was so tall, he was looking straight into Molly's face. His drool, dripping to the ground, shrivelled the weeds on the path.

Atacama called, "He's a deephound! A faery dog! Be careful!"

Innes yelled, "Back off, Molly!"

Beth shouted, "We'll get you out."

Molly heard rattling and clanging, as her friends tried to force the gate open. She moved slowly towards them, but she didn't turn her back on the massive Crottel-dog. He grinned at her, his heavy snout wrinkled, then he growled: a fierce happy drumroll of a growl.

Molly changed into a hare.

She stood still, exactly where she'd shifted, staring at the beast towering over her.

The dog took one slow step towards her.

Molly knew she should run. But where? The last time Mr Crottel had set his dogs on her, she'd discovered there was no simple way out of this garden.

The Crottel-dog snarled and lifted his upper lip. He had very long, very sharp, nastily stained teeth.

Molly shivered. Was this how it was going to end? Mr Crottel was the witch who'd cursed her. Was he also the dog who would catch and kill her?

She wouldn't make it easy for him.

Molly started to run. She wasn't running towards safety, because there wasn't any safety in this garden. But she couldn't stay still while this dog bared fangs as long as her back legs.

He thundered after her, shaking the ground under her and huffing hot stinky breath above her.

She leapt round damp boxes, through scrawny roses and over weed-filled flowerbeds. But she was never out of the dog's sight long enough to hide amongst all the rubbish. She just had to keep moving.

Innes yelled, "The gate's locked, so Beth's making an escape route."

Molly could hear Beth's voice, calm and singsong, asking the twiggy winter hedge to untangle enough to let a hare through.

Molly heard the giant dog thudding behind her and the pet dogs barking inside the house. Then she heard Beth's voice become more demanding.

On Molly's next clockwise circuit of the garden, Beth's voice cracked into a panicky yell. "The hedge is refusing. He's strengthened it since the last time we were here, overridden the plants' natural desire to work with a dryad."

Molly ducked under a plastic chair and changed direction abruptly to run round the garden anti-clockwise. The dog slid in a clumsy circle, knocking the chair over, and followed her.

Then Molly heard a different thunder, a more musical rhythmic noise. The sound of hooves on a road.

As she ran past the saggy sofa cushions for the fourth time, Innes jumped over the hedge. The white stallion whirled round and faced the green dog.

Molly crouched behind the mouldy furniture and watched Innes and Mr Crottel square up to each other.

The horse was lower in the shoulders, though his arched neck lifted his head above the dog's head, so he was slightly taller. But the dog was twice as wide, and had acidic drool, nasty fangs and clawed paws.

Molly didn't want to watch Innes get hurt for her.

The dog leapt for Innes's long pale throat; Innes lashed out with heavy hooves.

The dog fell back.

Beth shouted, "Don't get distracted. Get her out of there!"

Molly realised Innes wouldn't leave without her, so she dashed from her shelter, towards the horse.

Innes kicked at the dog, to force him further away, then bent his left foreleg. Molly used it as a step, leapt to his withers and crouched there.

But she had no knees to grip with, no hands to hold the mane. So when Innes took a couple of fast steps,

Molly slid off, right under the nose of the sniggering green hound.

She rolled away from his fangs, only to feel other teeth close around her.

What had grabbed her? It wasn't the Crottel-dog, she could see him snarling and snapping, rushing forward at her and whatever held her. It wasn't one of Mr Crottel's other dogs either, they were still inside the house.

Her wide hare vision could see white hair, white legs.

Innes. She was in Innes's mouth, held by his long horse teeth and gentle horse lips.

She was safe.

But she didn't feel safe. This was what a hare feared most: to be prey in between jaws, feeling hard teeth and hot breath, knowing a hunter was about to bite down.

Molly was on the edge of panic. She wanted to jerk free and run straight at the green dog, just to get away from these teeth.

She fought the desire to writhe and escape. She hung in his mouth, as Innes whirled away from the snapping dog and leapt high over the uncooperative hedge.

As he crossed the boundary, Molly shifted from light hare to heavy human, and fell suddenly from his mouth.

She heard her coat rip, rolled when she hit the pavement and leapt to her feet. The green dog followed them over the hedge and landed on his clicking clawed paws on the road.

"Thanks Innes," she gasped, as he changed to a boy. Then she faced the green dog. "Mr Crottel," she said calmly, her hands spread out in front of her. "I'm sorry I didn't tell you what's happened to my curse. If you change back, I'll tell you."

The dog grinned, showing dark-green gums above his stained brown teeth. Molly relaxed her shoulders.

Then the dog growled, and she shifted again.

Molly realised Mr Crottel wanted to chase her more than he wanted to know what had happened to his curse. But she wasn't trapped in his garden any more. She had the whole of Craigvenie, the whole of Speyside, the whole of Scotland to run in.

She ran towards the fields, where her paws were most comfortable and her legs moved fastest.

Could she outpace this huge beast there?

She leapt into the first field, crashed to the ground as a girl, and shifted back to a hare as fast as she could. Then she ran again. She felt her paws fly across the hard frosty earth.

As a hare, Molly was faster than a horse. She'd proved that, to Innes's embarrassment, in many races over the last few months. She was faster than a dog too, even a greyhound, so long as she kept the dog off-balance by changing direction unpredictably. She was faster than almost anything on four legs.

But this dog was huge. He wasn't really a dog – not a pet dog or even a hunting hound. What had Atacama called him? A deephound? He was a magical dog. A monstrous dog.

A dog who was shaking the earth as he chased her.

A dog who was keeping up with her.

Perhaps she could tire him out. It must be exhausting, moving that bulk around, under that thick dog hair. So she ran uphill and downhill. She ran in spirals and circles. She leapt walls and squeezed under fences, shifting back to a hare each time a boundary turned her human.

The beast's breath got noisier, and his smell, whenever she doubled back and crossed his path, got sweatier and more pungent. But he still kept up with her.

Then Molly leapt a wall separating one farm from another. She became a girl again, sprawled on the ground, as the dog cleared the wall easily, just metres to her left.

Her plan wasn't working. She would have to leap over houses to tire this thing out...

Perhaps he would leave her alone if she stayed a girl. Perhaps it was her hare form he wanted to chase, not her human form. She stood up on her denim-clad legs.

The dog lurched towards her, jaws open wide.

She stumbled backwards and the dog's fangs closed on her ankle, on her thick brown winter boot. She felt the painful squeeze of the dog's jaws and smelt the leather burn as the dog's drool slid down it.

The dog opened his mouth to take another bite, higher up her leg, above the protection of her boot. While his jaws were open, Molly shifted into a hare, and ran again.

So that plan wouldn't work either. This deephound, this green stinking monster, was happy to eat humans as well as hares.

She couldn't let those jaws get so close again.

Chapter Five

Molly ran, sprinting and leaping, keeping just ahead of the massive green dog who'd apparently decided to end her curse by ending her life.

Then, behind the crashing thumps and rattling breath of the beast pursuing her, Molly heard new noises. The sharper, cleaner noise of a horse galloping. And Beth's voice.

"Molly!"

She saw the black-and-purple shape of Beth on the white blur of Innes, edging into her almost-360-degree field of vision. Innes and Beth were chasing after the dog chasing her.

She didn't stop, she didn't turn round. She just kept running.

"Molly!"

She wouldn't lead this monster back towards her friends. She kept running away from them.

"Molly! Head for my woods. I can protect you there."

Molly still didn't alter her speed or direction. She didn't want Beth to put herself at risk.

"I can protect us *all* there," Beth yelled, faintly.

That was useful to know. Somewhere they would all be safe from this beast's size and teeth and burning dribble.

If Molly ran directly towards the woods now, her hunter would know where she was going, and might be able to cut her off. So she ran in the other direction.

"No, Molly!" shouted Beth. "Head for the woods!"

But Molly *was* heading for the woods. She was heading there hare-style, going the long way round.

She ran across clumpy winter earth and scraggly winter grass. The dog ran after her. She jerked and jinked, leapt and dodged, always circling round towards Beth's woods.

Then she realised there was a river ahead of her.

She could swim, as both a hare and a human. But this river was a boundary. Changing as she leapt over a wall was bad enough. Changing as she crossed a river would slow her down a lot more.

It was the only way to get to safety, though.

She hurtled down to the river's edge, choosing a route under jaggy brambles, hoping the thorns would slow the deephound. Then she leapt towards the far bank.

She was only a quarter of the way across when she splashed into the freezing water, soaking her muddy jeans, burnt boots and ripped coat.

The dog jumped in after her.

Molly scrambled to her feet. There was no point becoming a hare, because a hare couldn't move faster than a girl in shallow water on a slimy riverbed.

She backed away from the dog, her boots slipping and slithering on wobbly stones and slick waterweed.

The dog lunged at her, his drool hissing as it hit the peaty river. He was snapping and biting, but he wasn't snarling and growling. Perhaps he'd prefer to bite her as a girl. A girl would make a bigger meal than a hare…

Molly took another step backwards, out of his reach and out of the river. Now she was on dry land, with firm footing. She could run. But she had no time to shift. The dog leapt forward again, mouth wide open, teeth bared.

And Molly punched him on the nose. One fast hard whack with her fist, right on his delicate pale-green nostril.

The dog stopped in surprise. A string of yellow drool swung up and hit Molly on the back of her hand, burning her skin.

Molly willed herself back to her hare form. She ran from the startled dog, who, after one silent moment, thundered across the ground behind her again.

Now she could see Beth's trees, not too far ahead. In a short sprint, no dog could catch her. Not at full speed.

She didn't want to run at full speed, because her right forepaw was still stinging from that nasty drool.

But she didn't want to be eaten either.

So Molly ignored the pain and concentrated on the trees ahead, all dressed in their dull dark winter colours.

She could see two silver birch trees bending towards each other, like they were being pushed by strong winds blowing in opposite directions. The trees curved inwards, their smoky-purple branches mingling and weaving together, creating an arch.

On the other side of the linked birches, the wood was lit by a brighter warmer light than the rest of the dreich February landscape. The trees that Molly could see through the arch were radiant and shimmering. The birds fluttering round them were shadowy, less vivid. It looked to Molly as if the trees were carefully painted with gleaming enamel and everything else was hastily sketched in dusty chalk – as if the trees were more alive than the birds.

Behind her, she could hear the dog growling and snarling, snapping and thundering. She ran, as fast as she ever had.

And the hare reached the trees before the dog reached the hare.

As Molly crossed into the wood, she shifted and stumbled forward in her human form towards the two linked birch trees. A pale hand appeared from nowhere and dragged her through the arch into another world.

She was surrounded by bright brown and clean green, with the cool blue sky curving high over her and the damp sustaining earth stretching deep below. She was in a world of height and depth, wind and water.

This was still Beth's wood. The same trees, in the same place. The same roots and paths on the ground. But it felt different. The world was steady, and calm, and full of everything she needed. The sky. The air. The earth...

"Molly!" whispered Beth. "Molly. Concentrate. We're all here."

She looked round. They were all here. Beth. Innes. Atacama. They were really close to her, but she hadn't noticed them. Beth's pale skin, purple hair and green eyes were sharp and clear, full of power and energy. But the others were a bit hazy. A bit irrelevant...

Molly moved her head, gently flexing.

She saw the beast that wanted to eat her, in the distance, even hazier than her friends. Oh, look, there he was. Running closer. Running straight towards the arch.

Running straight towards Molly.

She smiled. She felt a breeze and knew it would soon bring a cloud of delicious rain. Then the cloud would move on, the sun would glow and all would be well.

The dog ran closer and closer.

"You're in the trees' world," whispered Beth. "You're quite safe. Don't worry."

Molly wasn't worried. There were worms under the roots. All was well.

"The trees can't see or hear or smell, so when we're here, we can't be seen or heard or smelt. Don't disturb any branches and you'll be fine."

Molly was fine, as she watched the dog come even closer, sniffling and snuffling. He was still out of focus, not as clear or important or solid as the white water-bearing clouds above the twigs.

Molly felt a strong itching urge to stretch upwards

and downwards, and she pushed her fingers into the welcoming earth.

Beth grabbed Molly's wrist and pulled her hand gently out of the earth. "Stop it. You're not a tree."

Molly grinned. Everything was a tree, really, wasn't it? Everything important.

"She's going native," said Innes. "She wants to be a tree. She's gone tree-crazy."

"The first time we visited Beth's world," said Atacama, "you tried to plant your toes."

Innes smiled. "I was three. I liked playing in mud."

Molly tried to speak, to say that Innes still liked playing in mud. But really, it wasn't that important. Who needed words, when it was going to rain soon?

The dog was still sniffling and snuffling. He was taking up too much space in the woods. And he was the wrong kind of green: an artificial, chemical, diseased green. He didn't fit.

As the dog bounded hugely and rudely round the trees, hunting for a scent trail he wasn't going to find, Beth said, "Molly, your hand is hurt!"

Atacama said, "The deephound's drool must have burnt her."

"Is she bitten as well?" asked Innes.

Beth gasped. "There are toothmarks on her boot! He might have savaged her. Molly! Are you injured? Snap out of it, Molly. Talk to me. You could be bleeding to death under that red jacket." Beth started to unzip Molly's coat.

Molly said, "No." Fuzzily, like her tongue was heavy and unnecessary. "No. Just my hand. Not bitten. Just dribbled on. When I punched the silly green dog."

Innes laughed quietly. "Well done! He is a silly green dog, isn't he? A big daft dog who needed punched."

"Don't encourage her," said Beth. "Molly, give me your hand."

Beth wrapped a papery length of pale-green lichen round Molly's injured hand, then hummed gently.

"Healing magic," murmured Innes. "I'd forgotten Beth could heal more strongly in the trees' world. That's why trees allow dryads in—"

"It's why trees *create* dryads," said Atacama. "They're a link, to stop the trees forgetting... forgetting the wider world, and they're a conduit for the healing power of the earth. Dryads work for trees, not the other way round."

Molly's hand felt better. Her head became a little clearer. She noticed more than just sky and earth. She could see other beings in the woods: grey forms on the ground, rooting beside plate-like fungi; a yellow shape in the air, fluttering over spiky daffodil shoots. She could sense new growth under the empty patches where a witch's curse had killed life in these woods for so many years, before it was lifted.

Beth patted Molly's injured hand. "Is that better?"

"Yes. Thanks. But... how did you know... where I would run?" She waved vaguely at the arch Beth had pulled her through.

"I didn't know." Beth gestured all around her, and Molly

45

saw lots of birch trees bent into arches. "I turned every birch pair at the edge of the wood into a door. I'd better close them now."

Molly watched Beth release the nearest pair of trees, and sighed as the birches stretched gratefully back up to the sky.

Then Molly saw something else. A small figure with black and orange fur. No. Black hair and an orange cardigan. A person. A child. Dancing and skipping. Running up behind the green dog.

Rosalind, Molly thought. She was fairly sure the small girl shouldn't run up and dance around the green dog. Why? Ah, yes. Because the girl was Beth's cousin, and because the dog wasn't friendly.

Rosalind, Molly said, almost out loud. She should really warn someone.

Innes was lying down, dozing in the calmness of the trees' world. Atacama was frowning, as if he was trying to remember something. Beth had her back turned, closing the doors on the far side of the wood. And the little girl was bouncing up and down just behind the monstrous dog.

"Rosalind," Molly said, actually out loud this time.

Beth turned round, Innes sat up and Atacama looked alert again.

The little girl grabbed the green dog's ragged tail, waggled it once, giggled, then skipped between two rowans to enter the trees' world.

The dog spun round and sniffed the empty ground.

Rosalind bounced towards Molly, not disturbing a dry leaf or a low branch, but filling the whole space with smiles and giggles.

"Hello! You're all in my world! Isn't it lovely! I feel taller when I'm with my trees. I feel like I could touch the sky." She reached up and grinned.

Molly could see the confused dog sniffing the nearest trees.

"I might be able to touch the sky once I'm five. And I'm five on Monday. Will you come to my party? Molly, Innes and Atacama, will you all come and play hide and seek, and pin the berry on the branch, and find the fungus fairy, and musical toadstools, and what's the time Mr Fox? Atacama, your little sisters are coming, so you could help me teach them to *fly*!"

Rosalind flung her arms out and birled in a circle. Beth pulled her down and gave her a tight hug. "Careful. We don't want the dog to know where we are."

"That big smelly green dog? Are you playing hide and seek with him?"

"It's not a game. The dog wants to hurt Molly."

"Bad dog!"

"So let's wait quietly until he goes away."

Rosalind nodded, then leant over to whisper loudly in Atacama's ear. "If you come to my party, you have to bring me a present. Because you're all friends, you can bring the same present. You could go on a quest, like you did last year, to find me a special present!"

Beth said, "You can't invite people to your party just to get presents from them."

"Why not?"

Innes smiled. "Why not indeed? I'd be delighted to come, and I'll definitely bring you a present."

Rosalind grinned. "Molly, will you come too?"

Then the dog howled in frustration, and started to chew on a stick.

But the stick wasn't fallen dead wood. The stick was a living birch tree. The dog wrapped his jaws round the slender trunk and shook his head violently.

Beth yelled, "Stop that! Now!" She sprinted through the final birch archway and attacked the huge green dog.

She ran up behind him. "Leave that tree alone, you horrible brute!" The furious dryad grabbed the dog's scabby left ear and hauled down on it hard.

The dog opened his jaws and backed away from the tree, then he whirled round and bit at Beth.

Chapter Six

Molly was a hare again. The moment the dog howled, Molly had shifted. She sat up on her haunches and saw the huge green dog spin round to savage her friend.

But Beth wasn't standing beside him any more. She was standing in a tree, balanced on the black branch of one of her tallest birches.

"Sit!" she called. "Stop biting and sit down, you trespassing beast."

The dog snarled at her.

And every tree in the wood turned to look at the dog.

Molly knew that the trees didn't have eyes, or fronts and backs. The trees didn't even move. But suddenly it was clear that every single tree was watching the dog, that the massive weight of all the solid timber in the wood was focussed on him.

Beth leapt down from the tree. "I said *sit*."

The dog sat.

Molly started to feel anxious, as she watched the dog and the dryad staring at each other. She wasn't worried about Beth, who looked more powerful and confident than Molly had ever seen her, backed up by all these trees. Molly was becoming anxious just sitting in the wood.

In the trees' world, everything was static. Everything was rooted, stuck down, held tight by the earth.

Trees don't run or even walk. Trees don't have escape routes. Trees just stay where they are and take whatever comes at them: violent wind or violent dogs or even fire. Trees don't run.

But Molly needed to run. Even when she was sitting still, she needed to be sure which way she could run if she had to. Here in the trees' world, safe beside Atacama and Innes, with Rosalind laying out a mosaic of twigs and pinecones by her paws, Molly still needed to know the way out. But Beth had closed the last arch as she ran through it. There was no way out.

Molly felt her heart pounding faster. She was starting to panic.

She tried to concentrate on Beth, standing tall and dignified in front of the huge green dog. "You have bitten one of my friends. You have injured one of my trees. You are not welcome here. I banish you from this wood forever."

Molly watched the suddenly pathetic-looking Crottel-dog nod.

"You will promise never to damage a tree or threaten one of my friends again. Or by the power of these trunks and branches and roots, I will return you to where you came from, back to your roots."

The dog whined and sank at Beth's feet in an apologetic heap of mouldy green hair. Then the heap shook itself into the form of a cringing man.

Mr Crottel whimpered, "No! Don't send me back…"

"Then get out of my woods and promise to leave my trees and my friends alone."

Beth leant over him, her body bent like a tree in the wind. Molly saw all the trees in the wood bend with her. All curving towards him, all threatening him.

"Yes! Alright! I'll go now." He stood up and stumbled towards the edge of the woods, all the trees watching him go.

"Promise me," boomed Beth, her voice echoing off the trees, "or I will send you back to your roots."

"I promise." He started to run. "I promise I won't bite a tree again."

"And my friends."

"I promise I won't bite your true magical friends either."

He ran out of the woods. As soon as he was beyond the reach of Beth's branches, he laughed. "But your human friend is still fair game!" He dropped to all fours and loped towards the snow-topped mountains, running on his human arms and legs, still wearing his greasy suit.

Beth wrapped her arms around the broken birch and leant her head against it.

Innes stood up and walked forward. But his steps didn't take him anywhere. He couldn't get past the nearest tree. "Rosalind, how do we get out?"

"Why do you want to get out? It's nice in here. Trees are kind and friendly."

"It *is* nice in here," said Innes, "but Beth is out there and she's upset, so she needs her friends."

Rosalind looked up. "Her tree is hurt. Poor Beth!" She spoke politely to a pair of rowans, which bent into a door.

Innes stepped forward. But Molly beat him to it. As usual. She was out into the greyer harder flatter world in two leaps.

This was her world. The earth no longer seemed like a generous depth, it was a surface for running on. The sky no longer seemed like a friendly height, it was an emptiness where danger could swoop down on fast wings. The trees were just trees, and the people were in sharp focus.

In this world, she had an exit strategy. She ran to the western edge of the wood, tumbled to the ground as a girl, and looked round.

Beth was crouched by the injured silver birch, sobbing. Rosalind was sitting beside her, patting the tree, then patting Beth, then patting the tree again. Innes and Atacama were standing supportively nearby.

Then Beth stood up, walked between two trees and disappeared. Rosalind followed her.

"She can heal the tree faster and more effectively from inside the trees' world," said Atacama. "The process is called... what's it called...?"

"I've no idea," said Innes. "First aid for foliage, perhaps?"

Atacama frowned, wrinkling his smooth black forehead. "There's a word for it…"

"Beth doesn't need to know the word to do the magic. Are you ok, Molly?" asked Innes. "How's your hand?"

"I'm fine." Molly looked at her hand. The lichen bandage had slipped off when she shifted. There was a red mark, but it didn't hurt any more.

"So what will you do about your curse now?" asked Innes. "Mr Crottel won't lift it unless you force him. And when he's that huge dog thing he won't be easy to defeat. What did you call him, Atacama? A faery dog?"

"That's what humans used to call them, when they thought anything from another world was 'faery'. They called them Cu Sidh, Dogs of the Shee, Faery Dogs. But can you imagine a glamorous faery queen taking a monstrous matted lump like that for a walk? They're not really faery dogs. There's a more accurate name for them…"

"You also called him a deephound," said Molly.

"Deephounds, yes. They're from the deeper layers, under the earth. They guard what humans call the… the underworld. They guard it, but they're also trapped there themselves. They're only allowed to enjoy sunlight once a year. At mid… At mid-something…"

"So, Mr Crottel is really an escaped deephound," said Innes. "Can they all take human form?"

"I've never heard of it before," said Atacama.

Innes shrugged. "Perhaps he stole the power to shift between the two forms, or perhaps someone trained him.

Maybe he prefers his human form to his original dog shape. He certainly didn't want to go back home, did he? He went all whiny when Beth threatened to return him to his roots."

"Why wouldn't he want to go home?" asked Molly.

"I think he's small, for a deephound," said Atacama. "Maybe he's the littlest in his family, the... em... Maybe he got bullied..."

"The runt of the litter, you mean?" said Innes. "If he's a runt, I wouldn't want to meet his brothers and sisters."

Molly looked at the tree damaged by the deephound. It was straightening, very slowly. The bend in the trunk, the splinters of wood, the rips in the bark, were all easing back into place.

Molly asked, "How long will Beth need to fix the tree?"

Innes shrugged. "We saw her fix a whole tree once before, didn't we Atacama? She only has a wee while until the wood hardens and can't be repaired. Do you remember how long it took?"

Atacama shook his head. "I don't... Are you sure I was there?"

Molly stared at the sphinx. She thought about his half-finished sentences and odd answers in the last five minutes. She knelt down beside him and asked gently, "What are you guarding these days? Are you guarding the Promise Keeper's door behind the distillery?"

"No, I'm guarding a lesser door. But... where? I was there yesterday. But I can't remember..."

Innes crouched down too. "Atacama, what's going on?"

Molly said, "Can you ask me your new riddle, for your new door?"

The sphinx didn't say anything.

Innes shook his friend's furry black shoulder. "Atacama, what's your riddle?"

"I can't remember my riddle. I can't remember anything..."

Molly looked at Innes. "It's his curse. It's come back."

Atacama roared in despair and threw himself to the ground.

And Molly turned into a mountain goat.

Molly didn't realise she was a goat. She knew she was balancing on four hooves, but she didn't know exactly what she was.

Atacama knew what she was. The sphinx looked up and she saw a flash of recognition in his eyes.

And Innes knew what she was. He laughed. "A goat? Really?"

Then her friend Atacama – wise, sensible, kind Atacama – leapt at her.

So Molly ran.

The goat form was fast and nimble on the root-strewn paths. But not fast enough.

Molly felt a crunching weight land on her back.

She bleated with panic, but she didn't slow down, despite her terror and the extra weight over her back legs. She sprinted to the edge of the trees.

Just as the weight shifted forward and she felt the hot breath of a hunting cat on her neck, she rolled to the ground as a girl and knocked the sphinx off with a hard swipe of her elbow.

Atacama gasped. "Molly? Is that you? Did I chase you?"

She nodded.

"I'm sorry! But I saw a goat. And that's what sphinxes hunted in the old stories. I forgot you were my friend. I forgot I shouldn't..."

"You forgot you shouldn't eat her. Whatever shape she is." Innes pulled Molly up. "So, we have a girl who changes into all sorts of inconvenient prey, and a sphinx who can't remember his friends or his riddle. Is that a fair summary of how weird our day has been?"

Molly nodded, as they walked back to Beth's tree. "It's as if both our curses have become more *powerful*. I used to shift to a hare when I heard a dog, now I shift to prey when I hear any predator. Atacama forgot one riddle last autumn, now he's forgetting—"

"Everything," moaned Atacama.

Innes sighed. "And my dad being a rock became him splitting into gravel."

"You've already lifted his curse," said Molly, "so it can't do any more damage. Mr Crottel won't lift my curse, unless I learn to defeat him. But it should be easy to get the curse-caster to lift Atacama's—"

"Of course! We never broke Atacama's curse, just found a way round it. We can fix this, Atacama. We'll ask your curse-caster to lift it!"

"And I'm sure he will lift it," said Molly, "because he apologised to you for setting the curse, then saved our lives several times last year—"

"Don't give him all the credit!" Innes grinned. "We saved his life, too."

Atacama looked at them. "But who... who cast...?"

Molly could see confusion and fear on the sphinx's normally calm face as his memories slipped away.

She gave him a hug. "Don't worry. When we all met on the curse-lifting workshop, we didn't bother lifting yours, because it was easy to get round. We made up a new riddle, remember?"

Atacama shook his head.

"And when we broke the toad's curse, he turned into Theo, the elemental magician who'd cursed you. Theo came with us to the Promise Keeper's Hall, where we found the cute little baby who maintains curses, and the nasty childminder Nan who was giving power to her own curse-hatched children by burning the baby back to a newborn every night. We teamed up with Theo, remember...?" – Atacama frowned – "...to defeat Nan and let the baby grow up. Theo should have his power back, now that the hair Nan shaved off has grown, and if we tell him his old curse is causing problems, I'm sure he'll lift it."

Innes added, "With his great big brain and great big ego, I'm sure he'll also have lots of fancy theories about why this is happening."

Molly nodded. "He might even suggest a way to stop it." She stroked Atacama's ears. "We'll get your riddles back, and everything else. Where is Theo? Anyone know?"

Atacama shook his head again.

Innes said, "Last time I heard from him, he was—"

Beth stepped out from behind the bent tree, her eyes red from crying. "I couldn't heal her completely. She was too damaged by that vicious hound. She'll live and grow, but she'll always be scarred and crooked. And it's all my fault. I shouldn't have offered my trees as sanctuary. I shouldn't have led that beast here. I shouldn't concern myself with the world outside the wood."

"I know it hurts," said Innes. "I suffer when my rivers are blocked or polluted. But now we have to leave your woods, so we can find Theo and ask him to lift Atacama's old curse, because Atacama has started forgetting things."

Beth said, "No. My duty is to my trees, not to anyone else."

"I don't remember everything," said Atacama, "but I do remember that you promised to help Molly lift her curse."

"What use is my promise when she clearly doesn't want to lift her curse? Whenever we try to help, she backs away." Beth glared at Molly. "You don't want to break your curse, do you? You'd rather be a worm occasionally than lose your power to run and jump. You'd rather be a rat occasionally than lose a race to Innes. You've allowed the curse to become who you are, Molly Drummond, and I can't put my trees at risk to keep a promise you don't want me to keep. Anyway, you released us all from that vow last year, when Innes turned out to be a curse-caster."

Molly didn't want to argue with Beth when the dryad was clearly upset, so she nodded. "It's ok, Beth. You don't have to help me. But Atacama needs his friends right now, to go with him to ask Theo to lift the curse."

"You don't need me for that. Theo will be happy to help Atacama, however many of us go. But my trees do need me, so I'm staying here. I won't lead any more monsters back here just to help a gang of curse-casters and curse-lovers. I can't let you drag me any closer to dark magic. I must put my trees first."

She sat by her wounded tree and folded her arms.

"That's just silly and selfish," said Innes. "We aren't dragging you towards dark magic, we're trying to free Atacama and Molly *from* dark magic."

"Says the kelpie who cursed his own father, and is about to visit a magician who regularly uses curses as tools? You lot paddle in dark magic all the time. I'm not staying with you while you drown in it. And I'm not letting you flood my wood with it."

Molly said, "It's fine, Innes. We're only going to see Theo, we can manage without her."

Beth leant her head against the scarred trunk and closed her eyes.

Molly said gently, "And I will prove to you, Beth, even if you're not there to see it, that I really do want to be free of dark magic."

Molly led the way out of the woods, away from the faint sound of Rosalind singing, "Happy birthday to me..." and the even fainter sound of Beth sobbing.

Then they went in search of the most powerful magic-user that Molly had ever carried in her pocket.

Chapter Seven

As they walked away from Beth and her wood, Molly asked, "So where is Theo?"

Innes frowned. "I haven't actually seen him since Hogmanay. He's gone on some kind of retreat, researching an obscure magical project, and can't be distracted. He's written to me, though..." He pulled a crumpled parchment from his back pocket, flattened it and started to fold it carefully. "He's mostly been writing to me from this library. It closed down, but still has shelves and a few books, so it's handy for staying hidden and doing his homework."

Innes showed Molly and Atacama the top right-hand corner of the parchment:

Lumpy mattress
Near the lavatory
Basement
Aberrothie Library (closed)
By Aberrothie Primary School

Speyside
Moray
Scotland
British Isles
Europe
Earth
Solar system
Milky Way
Universe
Multiverses
Infinity

Molly laughed. "I used to do that too, but I stopped at 'universe'. So he's nearby?"

Innes nodded. "I hope so. It's less than half an hour at a reasonable canter. You can both run beside me."

Molly glanced back at the edge of Beth's wood. "I probably shouldn't use my curse just for convenience." She looked at Atacama. "Also, he might forget who I am and try to snap my spine again."

"So you can ride and Atacama can run."

Atacama looked up. "Run? To where?"

Innes sighed. "Never mind. Just stay close." He whispered to Molly, "Make sure he doesn't forget to follow. And watch out for a big grey stallion too, in case my dad is already healed and hunting me."

Innes turned into a horse and Molly clambered up. They cantered across the fields and through a sudden shower of sleety rain. Molly had to call to Atacama a couple of times, reminding him to keep close.

When they reached the fence at the back of Aberrothie Primary, Innes leapt over, landing just beyond a big oval puddle on the cracked tarmac.

As Atacama scrabbled up the fence, Innes shifted back into a boy. He stared at the edge of the puddle and said, "Wet footprints."

"I don't see any," said Molly.

"Whoever left them splashed water about to cover them. But you can still see a heelprint here and a toeprint there." Innes looked round. "That's the library, at the side of the school. The footprints go in the other direction, to that bike shelter."

He walked cautiously towards the long wooden shelter, which was open on one side, and patchy with peeling green paint. Molly followed and urged Atacama to join her.

Innes pointed at a scattering of paint flakes at the base of one of the posts holding up the sagging roof, then touched a scrap of grey cloth impaled on a splinter just above shoulder height.

He whispered, "Someone climbed the fence, landed in that puddle, covered their trail and climbed onto the roof. Someone is hiding here."

"It might not be anything to do with us," Molly whispered back. "It might just be local kids, playing."

"Can we take that risk?" Innes pulled the fabric off the wood and held it out. "Atacama, sniff this."

"I am not a dog!" snapped the sphinx.

Innes smiled. "You could forget everything else in the world and still be absolutely sure you're not a dog, couldn't you? I know you're not a dog, but you have a better sense of smell than me or Molly. So, sniff, please."

Atacama sniffed the scrap. He sniffed the paint. He lifted his head towards the roof and sniffed the air.

The sphinx nodded. "I recognise the scent. It's someone I should warn you about, but I can't remember…"

There were lots of magical creatures Atacama should warn them about. But Innes could only focus on one.

"My father! Is it my father? Is he up there? Has he followed me? Is he about to attack me?"

Molly murmured, "How could he have followed you? Whoever's up there got here before us."

"Atacama, is it my dad's scent?"

But the sphinx just shrugged.

Molly had seen Innes face carnivorous sea monsters and eye-pecking crows with calm courage and sarcastic remarks. But right now he was scared. Not nervous, or worried, or wary. Actually scared. His hands were shaking, his breath was stuttering.

Molly said quietly, "Let's back away, over to the library."

"No. I can't walk away. Then he'd be behind me and I'd never feel safe. I have to deal with this *now*!"

Innes reared up as a huge white stallion and kicked the roof of the bike shelter.

The edge of the roof splintered and crashed down

around them in a shower of rotten wood, sharp slates and a falling grey figure.

Molly ducked out of the bike shelter, covering her head. As soon as the last beam had fallen, she stepped back in.

She saw a skinny girl in ragged grey clothes, holding a length of wood in one hand and a shard of roof slate in the other. Innes and Atacama were threatening the girl with their hooves and claws.

The girl slashed out with the broken slate. Atacama dodged out of the way. At least he hasn't forgotten how to move in a fight, thought Molly, as she ran forward, picking up a slate of her own. She stood between Innes and Atacama, pointing the sharpest edge of the slate at the girl.

The girl jabbed the spear of wood towards them.

Innes kicked and the wood splintered.

The girl threw the stump of wood away and jerked the slate forward again.

Molly said, "Don't be silly. There are three of us and only one of you. Put down your weapon, now."

The girl ran at Molly, waving the slate blade. Molly dropped down and rolled at the girl's feet, knocking her over. Atacama lashed out, swiping the blade from her hand. And Innes stood above her, one hoof raised over her head.

Molly stood up.

The girl lay on the ground, staring at them. She had a thin face, a sharp nose, big dark eyes and short shaggy black hair.

Atacama looked confused and Innes was still a horse, so Molly spoke. "You're a curse-hatched."

The girl at her feet nodded.

"You ambushed us last year. You helped tie my hands so I couldn't shift and escape. You stood and watched when Corbie threatened to kill my friends by pecking their eyes out."

The girl nodded again.

Innes crashed his hoof down, just millimetres from her head.

The girl curled up and started to sob.

Innes turned back to a boy. "Watch out! She might shift and fly away."

"No, she won't," said Molly. "When Theo ripped the coats and cloaks of the human curse-hatched, he took away their ability to grow wings. You're earthbound, aren't you?"

The girl sobbed louder.

Molly had a sudden cruel desire to ask Innes to make a sparrowhawk's call and turn her into a songbird, so she could flutter above this flightless crow-girl – just for a moment, just to remind the girl of what she had lost.

But instead Molly crouched down. "Stop crying and talk to us. What are you doing here?"

The girl sniffled. "I'm—"

They heard slate fragments crunch behind them.

They all looked round.

A tall dark-skinned boy stood in the watery sunlight, outside the tattered shadow of the wrecked bike shelter.

The boy was wearing pale linen clothes and sandals. He had thick glossy shoulder-length black hair and a grin on his face.

"What are you doing here? I'm meant to be on retreat, staying quiet, meditating on the music of the multiverses. And here you are, demolishing buildings in broad daylight! Let's get indoors and hope no one heard you."

Innes said, "It's not just us, Theo. We have a captive. You might not want to take her into your secret library."

Theo stepped into the shelter and looked down. "A wingless crow. She's not very big and she can't fly away. Anyway, the library isn't mine and it isn't secret. And, unfortunately, there are plenty of other closed libraries I could work in. Bring her indoors, before anyone else comes to investigate all that crashing and banging."

Molly grabbed the girl's arm and pulled her up. "Come on. It's ok, I promise we won't hurt you."

Innes snorted. "Don't make promises on my behalf." He stayed close behind the crow-girl and Molly as they crossed the playground.

Once they were inside the library and Theo had locked the door, Molly let go of the girl's cold goose-bumpy arm. The girl slumped down on the floor and started to cry again.

Innes sighed, loudly.

Theo crouched beside her and she flinched. He smiled gently. "I don't know what these local brutes have been doing to you, but I didn't attack you. There's no need to be afraid of me."

"You did attack me," she whispered. "You stole my wings. Last autumn."

"True. You were threatening to kill us at the time, so I thought removing your ability to shapeshift was a reasonable response. But right now you're in a nice safe library, and no one is going to kick you or bite you or cut you – Molly, put that slate down please – or cast any spells at you."

He looked up at Innes. "Where did you find her?"

"She was on the roof of the bike shelter. Watching you, perhaps, or waiting for us. We saw footprints and signs of someone climbing up. So I kicked the roof apart, she fell down, then attacked us with a slate and a spear of wood."

Theo frowned. "I told the crows to stay away from my friends. I told Corbie to keep his head down and stop interfering with the curse arc. So who are you and what are you up to?"

She didn't say anything, just stared at him, pale-faced and shivering.

"We know who she is," said Innes. "She's one of Corbie's little monsters. Feeding on curses and trying to take over the world."

The girl shook her head. "We aren't. We can't. Your magician ripped our wings, your hare killed our leader. We can't build an army now. But you're right. I am one of Corbie's little monsters and you probably should kick me or bite me or attack me with magic spells. Because I've been sent here to spy on you."

Chapter Eight

Innes grabbed Theo's shoulder to pull him away from the crow-girl. "Careful, she's a spy."

The crow-girl wiped her nose on the back of her hand. "I didn't say I was a spy. I said Corbie sent me here to spy on you. But I don't want to do what my big brother says, I don't want to be a spy or a soldier or even a curse-hatched." She looked up at them all. "Really. I don't want to spy on you." She sniffed again.

Molly found a dusty box of paper hankies on the reception desk and handed it to the crow-girl. "Whether you want to or not, you weren't very good at it. You didn't cover your tracks properly. And why did you come *here* to spy on us anyway? We didn't even know we were coming to Aberrothie until less than hour ago."

"Corbie thought once you realised your curses were charging up, you'd visit your most powerful friend for help. I waited near the magician's lair, hoping you'd arrive so I could spy on you. But also hoping you wouldn't arrive, so I didn't have to spy on you. I don't want to. I think you might be right. Maybe we are monsters, maybe we should be defeated..."

Innes said, "How were you going to tell Corbie what we're up to?"

The crow-girl pointed to the high windows. "There's always someone watching. There's always someone to carry a message."

Molly saw black specks dotted across the sky.

The girl asked, "What are you going to do with me?"

Molly said, "Why don't you just go home and tell Corbie you don't want to spy on us?"

The girl blew her nose. "I can't. He'd be angry with me. And he'd send another spy. Maybe I could stay here, with you, then he'd think I was doing my job and he'd leave me alone."

Innes laughed. "If we let you stay, so you can listen to us and watch us, we would be helping you to spy on us."

"But I don't *want* to spy on you!"

"Who is this girl and why is she crying?" asked Atacama.

"Haven't you been listening?" said Theo. "Have you forgotten to wash your ears recently?"

Innes said, "His ears are fine. It's his memory that's the problem. Can you tie this sneaky crow-girl up with magic, so she can't get away while we tell you why we're here?"

Theo shook his head.

"Don't be all gentlemanly about this. She's our enemy, she admits she was sent here to spy on us. We can't let her wander round your library."

"It's not my library, it's the village's library. And I can't restrain her with magic."

"Why not?"

"Because..." Theo pointed his finger at the curse-hatched and said firmly, "Stay there. Don't move." She flinched again and nodded.

Theo beckoned his friends over to the children's section, which was full of stained purple and orange cushions but empty of books, and he whispered, "I can't restrain her with magic, because I can't *do* magic."

Molly looked at his glossy shoulder-length hair. "But you can store lots of life-force in your hair now. Can't you use that?"

"That's the problem. My hair has grown back thicker and healthier, and it stores too much raw power, at an even higher potency. If I use any power, even the tiniest amount, I use too much. So any magic I do becomes a bit exaggerated, a bit... dangerous."

Innes grinned. "Dangerous. Excellent. Just what we need to deal with the curse-hatched."

"No, it isn't. Not unless you want me to flatten the Cairngorms and boil the Spey to steam as side-effects of a small spell." Theo sighed. "I'm so powerful that I'm powerless. It's like a riddle and you know I'm rubbish at riddles. So, I can't do magic. We'll just have to keep an eye on her."

"Or tie her up in a more traditional way." Innes ripped faded bunting from the edges of the nearest shelves and marched over to the girl, who was still sitting near the front door. "Get up."

She looked at him, lips trembling.

Molly followed him. "Get up before he gets really annoyed."

"Why is he so annoyed?"

"You wrapped him in elastic so he couldn't shapeshift, then threatened to peck his eyes out."

"Oh, yes. Sorry." She stood up.

Innes said, "Sit on that chair."

The girl sat on a whirly chair by a bare computer desk. Innes spun the chair, winding the bunting round her and the back of the chair. Then he walked off.

The girl looked at Molly. "Please..."

Molly shook her head. "You tied us up much tighter than that. We can't trust you and we can't be gentle. You're too dangerous."

The girl sniffed. "I'm not dangerous. I don't have any power at all."

Molly said, "Don't sniffle. You left the hankies on the floor." She walked away, leaving the girl wrapped in flowery bunting on a slowly spinning chair.

Molly joined Innes, Atacama and Theo in the non-fiction section. Innes was saying, "...so these curses seem to have more power, more energy, more general nastiness. We need you to lift Atacama's curse, then use your research skills to help us find out what's going on."

Theo frowned at Molly. "Mice, worms and goats? Have you been a toad yet?"

She grinned. "No amphibians so far."

"Don't try it. It's no fun. So, let's get your memory back, Atacama."

The sphinx looked up at him, vaguely.

Molly said, "But how can you lift the curse, if you can't do magic?"

"Undoing magic is different." He faced the sphinx. "I'm sorry I didn't do this before. You found such an elegant way round the curse, I considered it broken already."

He stood in a clear space, away from the shelves and armchairs, and lifted his hands to shoulder height. "I, Theodorus Ptolemy Hekau of the Alexandrian Order, hereby lift the minor amnesia curse from the sphinx Atacama of Speyside. The curse is... lifted." He raised his hands over his head.

Then he sat down, gasping for breath.

Innes asked, "Are you ok? Are you out of practice?"

"I haven't done magic for a few weeks, not since I accidentally... em... But even so, that took more power than I'd expect to use lifting a lightweight curse. It felt like the curse held more energy. Not like Molly's altered curse last year, where the curse was at the same level of magic but the rules had changed just enough to make her life more difficult and dangerous. This was like Atacama's curse had moved up a level, had more magical charge pumped into it. I've never read about that happening to curses, or any other promises." He stood up. "Perhaps your curse mirrors will show what's happened. We need to visit the Promise Keeper—"

Atacama laughed. "I remember everything! I even remember my original riddle. It's not as good as the one we made up!" He looked at the magician. "Thank you, Theo. But please don't curse me again."

"No, my friend, I won't. I doubt I'll curse anyone again. Who'd want to hatch another of those?"

They all turned round to look at the curse-hatched girl.

The bunting was curled on the floor round the empty chair.

"She's escaped!" said Innes. "Where's she hiding?"

"She isn't hiding." Molly pointed to the nearest window, where the girl was standing on a stool, staring up at the sky. She wasn't sniffling any more, but there were bright tears running down her cheeks.

Innes yelled, "Get down, crow-girl."

"I have a name, you know. I'm called Snib. I have a name, and I have brothers and sisters, and one of them just died. Her name was Ammie. And she died when you lifted that curse."

She jumped down and walked to Theo. "When you raised your hands, my sister died. I don't know where she was this afternoon. Perhaps she fell from a branch or a fence post, perhaps she fell all the way from the clouds. But she fell. And now she's dead."

She whirled round, looking at each of them in turn.

"We don't *want* to be like this, you know. We don't want to be tied to curses. I don't want to live on other people's anger and pain. I don't want to live in fear of my curse being lifted or broken, so I fall dead from the sky. Not that I can fly any more, since your bald-headed desert boy ripped my wings from my back."

Snib sat on the chair and started to wrap the bunting round herself. "Don't you want to tie me up again? So you don't have to be scared of me, while I sit and grieve for my dead sister."

Molly said, "I'm really sorry about your sister. But you can see why we have to be wary of you..."

Snib laughed. "Why? Because you so cleverly found me spying on you? I wanted you to find me! That's why I left a trail of obvious clues. I wanted you to know I was there! I thought you'd be nice to me, the way you've all been nice to Theo even though he cursed one of you, and to Molly even though she's human, and to Beth even though she wishes you weren't who you are, and to Atacama even though he didn't let you through the door, and to Innes even though he's a monster.

"You've all been kind and friendly to each other, even though none of you are perfect, so I thought you'd be nice to me too." She sighed, and tied the bunting round her tummy. "Even though you've not been kind at all, I still don't want to spy on you. Because I don't want to be like this. Most of us don't. It's horrible, knowing that when a good thing happens to someone else, one of us dies.

I'm happy for you, riddling cat, that you're not cursed any more. But when you got your memories back, my sister lost her life.

"Ammie thought she was safe, because you'd worked round your curse. When a victim learns to live with their curse, like you did, the curse-hatched crow can finally stop worrying. But now curses are being charged up, getting bigger and scarier, so victims are putting in more effort and taking greater risks to break or lift their curses."

Theo said, "Curses *are* charging up! Why? How?"

Snib shrugged. "Corbie doesn't tell me everything. But maybe I could help you discover where the extra strength of the curses is coming from, and help you stop it, because it's putting us at risk, just as much as the curse victims. Molly, your curse-hatched was safe until you became a mouse and a worm and a goat. You were happy as a hare, weren't you? And my brother, your curse-hatched, he's happy as a bird. So there was balance. But now, your charged-up curse is endangering him just as much as it's endangering you, because it's making you more determined to break your curse. And if you break your curse, my brother will die."

She looked up at them. "So, will you let me help you? Will you let me join you?"

Chapter Nine

"No!" Innes slammed his fist down on an empty desk. "No, you can't join us."

"What are you going to do with me, then?" asked the crow-girl.

Molly said, "We aren't going to hurt you. Are we?"

"No," said Atacama. "Of course we aren't going to hurt her."

"Why not?" snapped Innes. "She tried to kill us."

"We can't hurt her," replied Atacama, "because we don't know what her curse is, and we don't know what happens to a curse if you kill its curse-hatched. If she's linked to a curse that keeps a malevolent monster trapped somewhere safe, for example, then it's probably better she's alive and annoying us, than injured or dead, which might weaken or break the curse."

"I don't think it works like that," said Theo.

"Are you sure?" asked Atacama.

"Not completely sure. The link between the curse-hatched and their curses was created secretly by Nan, and no one has tested it scientifically."

Innes grabbed Snib's right wrist. He shoved her cardigan sleeve up, then twisted her arm slowly, letting the harsh fluorescent light shine on her pale arm. One long patch of skin glimmered.

Snib had the image of a key marked along her arm.

"You *are* locking something up," said Innes. "What's your curse?"

Snib eased her arm out of his grip. "Corbie has never told me, and I've never met my curse-victim. He or she could break my curse, anytime. I'll get no warning. I have to be ready to feel the curse break, to feel myself break, anytime. It's… it's hard to enjoy life, when you don't know—"

"This is ridiculous." Molly started to unwrap the bunting. "This girl is just as much a victim of curses as any of us. She says she wants to help and I think we should believe her. What could she tell Corbie anyway? We don't know what's going on, we haven't found anything out yet." She threw the bunting on the floor. "Snib, would you like to come with us to the Promise Keeper's Hall?"

"Yes." A wide smile brightened Snib's sharp face. "Thank you."

"Molly!" Innes pulled her away. "That's crazy. She's been sent here to spy on us. How can you trust her?"

"Because she's miserable. You can tell she doesn't like being a curse-hatched any more than you liked being a curse-caster or Atacama liked being a curse victim. If she wants to help, I think we should let her."

"What if she's really spying for Corbie?"

"We'll make sure that she doesn't learn anything which would help Corbie, and that she can't get any messages to him. I'm not daft, Innes, I just don't think it's sensible to assume everyone is our enemy."

"Last year that snivelling girl took part in an ambush designed to kill me. That's proof enough she's my enemy."

Molly sighed. "What's the alternative? You don't really want to hurt her, do you?"

Innes shrugged.

"Molly's right," said Atacama. "The crow-girl is a minor threat if she's a spy and could be a major asset if she's an ally."

Theo nodded. "Molly's definitely right. I'm sure Beth would agree that holding grudges isn't good for us: it draws us too close to dark magic. Where is Beth, anyway?"

"She's in a huff," said Innes. "Holding a grudge against us for getting too close to dark magic. She's staying with her trees."

Theo said, "Then there's a vacancy in our quest team. And a new applicant. Come on, Snib, let's go to the Promise Keeper's Hall!"

But it wasn't that easy. Molly refused to shift into a hare because she was determined to prove to Beth that she wasn't becoming her curse, Theo couldn't use his magic in case he exploded the whole village, Snib couldn't fly because Theo had stolen her wings, and they couldn't all fit on Innes's back.

So they took the bus.

Or three of them did. While Atacama and Innes headed home cross-country, Molly, Snib and Theo settled down on the back seat of the local bus to Craigvenie.

Snib said, "I thought a magical quest would be more... exciting. Faster. More dangerous. Less dependent on bus timetables."

Molly said, "I'd rather take the bus than be ambushed in the hills. Which has happened to me, occasionally."

"I've said sorry about that already."

"This isn't really a quest and it isn't really dangerous," said Theo. "We're simply visiting Mrs Sharpe and Estelle at the Promise Keeper's Hall. We'll have a chat and a quick look at the mirrors holding information about the charged-up curses. It's not a quest. It's a social call, with a bit of research thrown in."

He turned to look directly at the crow-girl. "In the meantime, Snib, tell us: what's Corbie up to? If he's sending out spies, is he continuing Nan's plan to build an army?"

Snib shook her head. "He can't. He's afraid of your power and of the threats you made when you attacked the strongest curse-hatched and stole our ability to shift into birds. He's keeping his head down, because you said if he didn't, you'd do something even worse. Though I can't imagine anything worse than losing my wings..." She stared out of the window.

Molly nudged Theo along to the other end of the backseat and whispered, "If that's what's keeping Corbie from getting ambitious again, we mustn't let her know you can't do magic just now."

They got off the bus two stops before the clock tower in Craigvenie, and found Innes and Atacama sitting in a slice of shadow by a warehouse. They all walked past the distillery to the cooperage yard, then strode between pyramids of strongly scented casks towards a door guarded by a golden spotted sphinx.

"Hello, Caracorum," said Innes. "No need to ask us the riddle for the hundredth time. The answer is: a baby."

Caracorum smiled. "No, it isn't. I have a new riddle."

Theo sighed. "I still don't understand the last one."

"When did you get a new riddle?" asked Atacama.

"Don't you know about the new riddles? Oh, of course not." She laughed. "You're still guarding the back door of that sweetie shop! It's only the top-level guards, the ones trusted to guard *this* door, who have new riddles. So you won't get through the door today."

Molly said, "Just ask your riddle, please. We solved the last one, we might solve this one too."

Caracorum spoke, in her haughtiest voice:

My perfect beauty is made to be broken,
I can be freckled, tanned or pale,
    whether I've seen the sun or not,

I contain gold, but I'm not a treasure chest,
I contain white, but I'm not a snowball,
I have a smooth shell,
    but you won't often find me at the beach
Unless a witch is sailing away in my cracked remains.
What am I?

Theo sighed. "That makes no sense."

"It will make sense," said Molly, "once we know the answer. Riddles are backwards that way." She nodded to the sphinx. "Thanks. We'll be back with our answer soon."

Molly led them round the corner. "Who has an idea to start us off? We usually manage by circling round the riddle. Any possible answers, however daft?"

Snib said, "I wonder—"

"You want daft answers?" asked Innes. "What about a goose? Or a duck? Or a quack? Or the sound of two hands clapping? Or a wasp?"

"Be serious. Could it be teeth?" Atacama bared his long fangs.

Molly frowned. "Why teeth?"

"White and gold could be teeth with gold fillings."

"But teeth aren't made to be broken," said Theo. "Oh, I have an idea. I hardly ever have an idea with riddles, but perhaps it's... snails. With smooth shells, but not at the beach."

"There are lots of snails at the beach," said Innes. "Whelks, in rock pools: they're sea snails."

"Are you sure?"

"Yes, desert boy. Trust the water guardian on this one. Sea snails. I've eaten them. It's not snails."

Molly said, "Not teeth, not snails. But that bit about the witch, sailing away…"

Snib said, "I think—"

"What can you sail away in?" asked Innes.

Atacama said, "You could sail away in a boat or a ship—"

"Yes!" said Innes. "A pirate ship, you could sail in that, and it would have stolen golden treasure."

"And the white?" said Theo. "And the freckles?"

Innes laughed. "Ok, so a pirate ship, with golden treasure, and freckly pirates having a snowball fight. There's your answer."

Snib said, "It's not that complicated—"

"I remember!" said Molly. "My gran must have believed in tiny witches, because she said witches could sail away in—"

"Egg shells!" shouted Snib. "It's an egg. That's what I've been trying to say!"

"Of course!" said Innes. "An egg is made to be broken, and it has yolk and white inside. But Molly, none of the witches I've met would sail away in one."

Molly shrugged. "That's what my gran believed. I still bash a hole in the bottom of my shell when I've finished a boiled egg, so a witch can't use it as a boat."

"An egg?" said Theo. "That can't be right."

"Why not?" asked Innes. "We all think it fits and you're

the worst at riddles. Turns out our curse-hatched is the best." He almost smiled at Snib.

Theo shook his head. "It's not whether it fits the riddle, I trust you on that. But the sphinxes agreed to use crow-proof riddles, to stop the curse-hatched influencing the Promise Keeper while she grew up. A riddle with the answer 'an egg' is the opposite of bird-proof." He looked at Snib. "How did you know the answer?"

"I hatched from an egg. I live in Stone Egg Wood. Eggs are something I know."

"Exactly. Crows know eggs. So why is 'an egg' the answer to Caracorum's new riddle?"

Atacama said, "Perhaps Estelle has grown up. She was bigger than Rosalind last time we visited. Who knows how big she is now. Remember, she's growing unnaturally fast, because of all the years Nan stole from her. The crow-proof riddle agreement was for while she was a child."

Theo frowned. "Perhaps."

Molly said, "If Snib's answer is correct, we can find out for ourselves."

They walked round the pyramid.

"Go on, Snib," said Innes. "It's your answer. You should get the glory if it's right, and the embarrassment if it's wrong."

Snib faced the spotted sphinx and said clearly, "The answer is: an egg."

Caracorum scowled. "Yes. You may pass."

She backed away from the door. Molly reached out and pushed it open. They stepped into the darkness beyond.

Chapter Ten

"I've never come in this way before," whispered Snib. "Isn't it terribly dangerous? I've heard there are monsters."

Molly took her hand in the darkness. "It's fine. We've been this way lots of times, and we've only been attacked once."

As they walked along the dark corridor, flaming torches flickered into life. Mosaics on the walls and floor glittered with patterns and fruit, then a few steps on, the mosaics glittered with men and weapons.

The mosaic soldiers stepped off the wall and blocked the corridor.

"Token," said the tallest mosaic man.

Molly said, "You know we're allowed in."

"Token," he repeated, in a bored tone of voice.

Molly murmured to her friends, "Beth usually carries the token."

Theo said, "I kept one, just in case." From a pocket inside his linen tunic, he pulled out...

A potato.

A small, wrinkled, sprouting potato.

"A seed potato from Mrs Sharpe's farm," he announced. "The token to enter while Mrs Sharpe is the Keeper's guardian."

"No." The mosaic man's blue pebble eyes glowed with sudden excitement. "That's not the token. There's a new token. Show the token or face your doom!"

Molly sighed. "We're not going to 'face our doom' this afternoon. We could just walk back out."

"Or Theo could rip you apart, like the first time we met," said Innes.

He winked at Theo. Theo shrugged, took a step forward and raised his hand.

All the mosaic men took a step back.

Snib said, "I might have a token. It's not a potato, but..." She pulled a triangle of silvery glass from her ragged grey dress.

The mosaic men nodded and moved aside to let Snib pass. Molly and her friends followed.

As they walked towards the door at the end of the tunnel, Theo asked, "Why did you have the right token, Snib?"

"Corbie gave it to me, when he sent me to spy on you. He said it might be useful."

Theo frowned again. "Corbie should *not* know the token to enter the Hall."

The door opened and they stepped out into a beautiful courtyard, surrounded by the arched windows and doorways of the Promise Keeper's Hall.

"Should we say hello to Mrs Sharpe and Estelle first, or look at the mirrors first?" asked Molly.

Atacama said, "Can't you hear them? They're in the Chamber already. We can do both at the same time."

They walked towards the tallest windows, hearing faint giggles as they crossed the courtyard.

Molly smiled. "She does love playing with her toys."

"I was here six weeks ago, and she was the size of a ten year old," said Theo. "She might be growing out of toys by now."

The giggles got louder, and Molly said, "She's playing with *something*."

They looked in a window and saw Mrs Sharpe, the white-haired witch who'd taught them how to lift curses, sitting in a corner. A lumpy length of mud-brown and mustard-yellow knitting dangled from her clicking needles and coiled in a woolly worm cast at her feet.

And they saw a gold-haired girl standing at a long white table covered in mirrors.

"She looks older than us now!" said Molly.

Estelle had been a teddy-cuddling baby last October, and a doll-hugging little girl at Christmas. Now she was a teenager. She was as tall as Theo, she was wearing a short tight dress and heavy boots, and she wasn't playing with teddies or dolls any more.

"At least she's taking her job seriously," said Atacama.

Because the Keeper was playing with the mirrors.

Molly noticed a few changes in the Chamber of Promises.

The long table was the same, but the mirrors weren't tidy in racks, they were scattered on the floor and chairs in wobbly piles of glass and handles. The knitting witch in the corner looked very traditional, but the wide flat-screen TV hanging on the wall was more hi-tech than Molly expected in an elemental being's hall.

Estelle picked up a mirror and gazed at her reflection, tipping her head to the side, adjusting her gleaming gold ringlets. She smiled, then licked her pearl teeth.

"Let's go in," said Molly.

"Wait," said Theo. "What's she doing now?"

They watched as Estelle put her slim hand on the surface of the mirror. Sparks floated around her fingers. The mirror absorbed the sparks and started to glow.

"What's the mirror showing?" said Theo. "I can't see from here."

"Look at the screen," said Atacama.

The huge screen glowed, then showed a picture of two boys, probably brothers, possibly twins, sitting on a bed in a small cluttered room. One of them opened his mouth to speak, and a small glittering green stone fell out and landed on his lap.

He looked at it in horror and knocked it onto the floor.

The other boy spoke one word, then clamped his hand over his mouth. He started to cough and splutter, then pulled his hand away. His lips opened and a beetle, with skinny black legs and shiny green wing-cases, crawled down his chin, dropped onto his lap and scuttled away.

Both boys shrieked. A blue gem and a blue beetle fell to the floor.

Estelle laughed. "Look! This is a really funny one! It used to be just when they lied. Now it's whenever they speak at all. I wonder whether the jewel brother will still support the insect brother if I ramp it up to cockroaches…?"

Mrs Sharpe squinted at the screen with dull eyes. "That's not very kind. Perhaps you should put your energy into tidying up, rather than playing with mirrors—"

"Stop nagging me, Mrs S. It's my hall, they're my mirrors, I'll do what I like."

Mrs Sharpe said, "But…" then glanced down at her stripy knitting, which was winding round her body and tightening round her neck. She closed her mouth.

Estelle used a remote control to turn up the volume. Now Molly could hear the clattering of jewels and the fluttering of insects. One of the boys yelled, "Stop talking!" as a line of pearls dripped from his mouth. Both brothers put their fingers on their lips and sat silently staring at each other, tears running down their faces.

"Well, that's boring." Estelle sighed. "Ooh! I know! Breathing!" She put her hand on the mirror again.

The boys started to splutter and choke, and opened their mouths to gasp in air. But with every out-breath, a nugget of gold or a moth or a ruby or a ladybird tumbled down. Soon both boys were crouched on the floor, coughing and retching.

Estelle giggled. "That's much more fun to watch than

anything the old troll who cursed them could have imagined!"

Everyone outside the window watched the girl laughing and the boys weeping.

Molly whispered, "So that's what happened to the curses."

Snib sighed. "The Promise Keeper is charging them up herself."

"Just for fun," said Innes.

Molly frowned. "Maybe she doesn't know they're real people."

"Mrs Sharpe must have told her," said Atacama.

They looked at the witch in the corner, with her sagging face and unfocussed eyes, being bullied by her own knitting.

Theo said, "Maybe she has. Maybe Estelle doesn't listen any more."

"Then we have to tell her." Molly walked round to the Chamber's doorway. "Hello, Estelle."

The slim girl turned, light glinting from the metallic coils of her hair and her solid blue gem eyes.

"Hello, Estelle. Do you remember me? I'm Molly. You cuddled me in October when you were a baby, and at Christmas we played hide and seek."

"I remember you, Molly. You used to be taller, and I thought you were pretty. But now I see you're short and plain. Have you brought me tribute?"

"Tribute? Em, no…" She glanced round at her friends, walking through the doorway to join her. "But we have brought important information, which is sort of like a tribute."

"Go on then."

Molly nodded. "Ok. The curses aren't toys. You're not watching a film or playing a game. Those boys are real, their pain and fear are real. When that boy is coughing up insects, his throat is hurting and his skin is crawling. All the victims in all the mirrors are real."

"Yes. I know."

"You know?"

"Obviously." Estelle rolled her eyes. "I know you're real, because I've met you, and I've seen your curse in its mirror. So I know those boys are real too, even if I haven't met them."

Molly frowned. "You know they're real, but you're still charging up their curses?"

"Yeah."

"Why?"

Estelle laughed. "It's my job. I'm meant to put my energy into curses."

"You're meant to maintain them," said Theo, standing beside Molly. "You're meant to put in just enough power to maintain the curse at the level the curse-caster intended. It's your role to ensure the rules are kept, and lift the curse when the time is right. You must keep this arc in balance so you don't destabilise the whole magical helix. You are the Promise Keeper."

"Yeah. I'm the Promise Keeper. It's my power and this

is what I choose to do with it. It's more fun this way. Not so *boring*. Not as boring as knitting or tidying. Look!" She giggled. "I didn't know that would happen! I charge them up, but I can't be sure what the curse will do. Look!"

Molly looked up at the screen. The beetles were attacking the boys, crawling onto their feet. Both boys were screaming, and more jewels and more insects were raining from their mouths. The jewels were vanishing moments after they hit the ground, and the insects were fading away, but not until they were halfway up the boys' legs.

Estelle laughed again.

"Mrs Sharpe?" called Molly.

The witch looked up. "Molly? Hello! How's your hare? Or are you a mouse these days? That must be a nice change..."

"Mrs Sharpe?" said Innes. "Are you alright?"

Estelle smiled. "Mrs S is fine. She kept nagging me, so I found an old curse someone had put on her after a disagreement over magical knitting patterns and gave it some oomph. Now when she nags me, her knitting strangles her. She's much less annoying! But she doesn't appreciate my Curse TV. I hope you will. Pull the chairs over, let's watch together."

Molly looked round. In the chaos, she saw three kinds of mirrors: ones with ordinary surfaces, ones with glowing surfaces and ones with fractured surfaces.

"Have you been breaking curses too?"

"Not on purpose. But victims often become really keen

to get rid of a curse that's been charged up. A few victims have already defeated their curse-casters, or done dangerous tasks to lift their curses, which means more broken mirrors and more dead crows. And the curse-hatched are so pretty when they fall. The light on the feathers, the descending spiral... The bird flies up alive and tumbles down dead. It's like a metaphor. For something. I'm sure I could write poetry about it, if I could be bothered.

"It's fun watching the curse victims suffer. It's fun watching the crows fall. Otherwise nothing happens here. So, sit with me! Mrs S, bring us popcorn and nachos. We'll have a sleepover and watch curses together."

Mrs Sharpe stood up, still wrapped in her stripy knitting, and shuffled to the door.

"Please, Estelle. This isn't what Keepers do," said Theo. "Being a Keeper is a huge responsibility, you have to take it seriously, not use it for entertainment."

"Oh, shut up about responsibility. Mrs S says this is just a phase and I'll grow out of it. Let's enjoy it while we can! I hardly ever have visitors." She smiled at Snib. "Though your brother has been sneaking in sometimes. Corbie loves watching the curses. He likes being helpful too. He's tightened up the Hall's security, he's even started to suggest which curses I should charge up. But it's my game, I get to decide. So, crow-girl, you sit and watch too."

Snib backed away from her.

Estelle frowned. "I order you to sit with me, crow."

"No!" said Snib. "What you're doing is cruel. You have to stop."

"No one talks to me like that." Estelle slammed her foot on the stone floor and the floor cracked. "You will join me, laugh at these pathetic victims, eat snacks with me and pick up my crumbs. But you will *not* tell me what to do."

"Someone has to tell you," said Innes gently. "You used to be so kind to your dolls and teddies. You could be kind to these people too."

"Kind is weak and boring. If you're going to be boring, Innes, just go away."

She laid her hand on the mirror again. One boy spat out a stag beetle, the other coughed as a jewelled choker forced its way out of his mouth. Estelle giggled.

Molly walked up to her and took the mirror from her hand. "No, Estelle. We can't sit and watch, because that would be cruel, and we can't leave, because that would be abandoning these poor people."

A voice called from the doorway, "Salty popcorn or sweet, my dear?"

"Both!" Estelle yelled. "And chocolate truffles." She grinned at Molly. "Or she could bring cheese for you to nibble as a mouse, or mud for you to squirm through as a worm..."

Molly put the mirror carefully on the table. "Please stop. Please take your extra power out of all these glowing mirrors."

"No. I don't want to. And you can't make me. No one

94

can make me!" Estelle's voice became louder, sharper, harder, and she lifted one hand. All the cracked and fractured mirrors, from all the broken curses, rose off the floor, floating up to Molly's head height.

"GET OUT!" screamed Estelle. The mirrors fell to the stone floor. They shattered, in an ear-bursting crash.

Shards of glass bounced high off the floor. But the shards didn't fall back down. The blades of glass danced in the air, glittering like dust in a sunbeam, though much bigger, much sharper.

"Get out! If you won't be my friends and enjoy my hobbies with me, then get out and leave me alone."

The glass daggers cut through the air towards Molly and her friends, slicing straight towards their scalps and eyes and faces.

Chapter Eleven

Molly and her friends ducked, and the slivers of glass swooped through the air just above their heads.

The cloud of broken glass swerved round and swooped back again, even lower, even closer. Molly dragged Theo and Snib under the table. Innes and Atacama crowded in with them.

The glass scratched across the tabletop.

"The Keeper is not going to listen to reason," said Theo. "We have to leave."

"But what about Molly's curse?" asked Atacama.

"And the threatened curse-hatched?" asked Snib.

"And the curse victims?" asked Molly.

"She's too powerful. We have to retreat, for now."

The glass fell to the ground with a smash, breaking into smaller brighter splinters. "Maybe she's changed her mind about attacking us," whispered Molly.

Then each skelf of glass stood up on its sharpest tip, and the shining fragments scraped along the stone floor towards the group under the table.

The glass gouged lines in the rock, making the just audible screeching sound of a fork on a plate of baked beans.

"She's not going to change her mind," said Innes. "We'd better run!"

They scrambled out from under the table.

Estelle yelled after them, "That'll teach you not to nag me!"

In the doorway, they collided with Mrs Sharpe. She dropped the bowls of popcorn and sweeties she'd been carrying in her wool-wrapped arms. "Dearie me," she said loudly. "I'd better tidy that up."

As Mrs Sharpe bent down to pick up the bowls, she whispered to Molly, "Ask the crow about the box. The box will stop the Keeper—" The wool round the witch's neck was creeping up to her face. She muttered, in a muffled voice, "Dearie me, what a mess... You'd better go, now."

They sprinted across the courtyard, running from the broken glass chasing them and from the Promise Keeper yelling, "Don't come back or I'll make every curse in Scotland so heavy that the land sinks into the sea!"

Molly heard glass scraping on stone behind them, as they ran down the white tunnel.

"Leaving in a hurry?" said the tallest mosaic man. "That's a bit suspicious."

"We don't need a token to leave," gasped Molly. "Let us past."

The mosaic man laughed and stepped out of the way.

As they crashed through the door into Craigvenie, Molly looked back and saw a new figure joining the mosaic men. A figure made of silvered glass fragments.

They stumbled and tripped to the ground in front of the perfectly posed Caracorum. Molly slammed the door shut, while Snib pulled Innes to his feet and Atacama untangled his claws from Theo's cloak.

Atacama said, "Tell me, sister, who gave you that new riddle? Was it Corbie, the crow?"

Caracorum smiled sweetly. "I don't know. I was given my instructions by the senior sphinxes. I don't ask awkward questions. That's why I sit beside a pyramid guarding this important door, while you sit beside a purple recycling bin guarding the back door of a sweetie shop."

Atacama stalked away from his smirking sister.

As his friends followed him between the pyramids, Innes said, "That trip to the Hall didn't go spectacularly well."

"Nonsense," said Theo. "We know much more about what's happening to the curses now."

"Corbie must know what's happening too," said Snib, "if he's watching those nasty images with the Keeper. I don't understand why he's encouraging her, when those charged-up curses are a threat to us as well as to you."

"But don't the curse-hatched grow bigger and stronger when she charges up a curse?" asked Molly. "Like the black eagle linked to the curse Innes cast on his dad?"

"Yes, he was bigger and stronger. And now he's *dead*

because Innes lifted the curse when he realised it was getting out of control."

"Perhaps Corbie will risk a small number of dead curse-hatched," said Theo, "if he can gain a large number of stronger ones. There will always be victims like Molly whose curse-casters refuse to lift their curses."

"I'm not a victim," said Molly. "When we find Mr Crottel, I'll give him one last chance to lift this curse and if he refuses again, I'll *force* him to lift it."

Innes grinned at her. "Are you going to claim your ancestors' power and become a witch to defeat him in magical combat?"

"I hope I don't have to." Molly sighed. "But perhaps there isn't any other way..."

"Let's sit down over there." Atacama pointed to a clump of silver birches at the edge of the nearest field. "Well away from my annoying sister. "

They clambered over the fence into the field behind the distillery car park. In the summer the field was stocked with half a dozen Highland cattle as background for tourists' selfies, but in the winter it was empty.

Once he'd settled down under the trees and scratched his left ear, Atacama said, "Here's what we know. The Promise Keeper is already a teenager and has decided to use her power to charge up curses. And one of those charged-up curses has turned Mrs Sharpe into a dottled old wifie with a knitting habit who can't stop the Keeper."

"*We'd* better stop her," said Molly.

Innes said, "We should set you up in combat against Mr Crottel first."

"We don't know where Mr Crottel ran off to, but he certainly wasn't heading back to his house. So let's concentrate on Estelle. If we can prevent her charging up curses, then mine should go back to normal anyway. How can we do that?"

"Did you ask her nicely?" asked the tree above Molly.

They all looked up.

Beth was sitting cross-legged in the branches of the tallest birch tree.

Innes said, "I thought you were staying in your wood from now on."

She shrugged. "I wanted to check you were alright. And I wanted a look at your new friend."

Snib smiled and waved.

Beth glared at her. Then she looked at Molly. "I'm not going to put my trees in danger, but I might have useful suggestions for you."

"Like stopping the big bad wolf by asking nicely," said Innes.

"Did you try? Politeness isn't always your strength, Innes."

Molly said, "We did ask nicely, when we saw her torturing a couple of boys with beetles. But she threw glass daggers at us. Polite isn't going to work."

"We need to weaken her," said Theo. "She has lots of excess energy, built up over those years when Nan was controlling her, which she's now pouring into those curses. If we can make her weaker, she'll need the extra energy for herself, so she'll have to remove it from the curses."

"How do we do that?" asked Atacama.

"I don't know. No Keeper has ever deliberately sent their arc off balance before."

"Can't we ask your family?" said Molly. "It's their job to keep the helix of magic balanced, so can't they fix the curse arc?"

"They're all busy at the moment, dealing with... with the effects of my last attempt to control my overgrown powers."

"Where are they?"

"In the Pacific. I sank an uninhabited island and set off a few volcanoes. They're all there trying to undo the damage. That's why I've been sent here to do obscure research in an empty library."

"I thought you wanted to be near us," said Innes.

Theo smiled at him. "That too. But mainly it's to keep me out of the way. So, we could ask my family to help, but we'd have to wait a month for them to finish what they're doing and return home."

"If we wait that long," said Snib, "Molly will have been eaten, and most of my brothers and sisters will have bulked up like bodybuilders, then dropped down dead. There must be something we can do ourselves."

"You can mind your own business." Beth's voice fell on them from above. "Our interference last October caused

101

this problem. If we hadn't saved the baby Estelle from the flames, she wouldn't be messing about with Molly's curse now. Just like the circling snake warned us, the helix has twisted the other way. We should stop interfering, before we make things even worse."

Molly lay down and looked up at Beth, sitting on a slim branch that wasn't bending under her weight. "Are you even really here?" asked Molly. "Or are you in the trees' world?"

"I'm always in the trees' world, now," said Beth. "Just like Innes should stay with his rivers, Atacama should stand by his door and that crow-girl should get back to Stone Egg Wood. Each of us should stay in our natural place."

"What should I do?" asked Molly. "Crouch in a field, wait for a predator and take my 'natural place' in its belly? I can't do that. And I can't forget those two boys coughing up beetles and jewels either. I'm going to stop Estelle. Theo, tell me where her strength comes from."

"Estelle, like all Keepers, draws her power from the Earth's elements, the fundamental particles that make up all matter on this planet: gold, iron, carbon, hydrogen, oxygen... I get my power from the life-force of the landscape around me. She gets her power from the life-force of the whole planet. So any weapon made of the Earth's elements will just make her stronger."

"See. It's impossible," said Beth. "You should all go home."

Suddenly, Theo grinned. "It's not impossible! All we

need is an element that isn't from Earth. A substance that isn't part of her strength. I've heard of this, once. The Keeper of the Transformation Arc was given cosmic dust as a gift and was ill for years, like he had magical flu. If we bring Estelle into direct contact with something that isn't made of her own elements, it will weaken her."

"You're sure about that?" asked Molly.

Theo thought for a moment, then nodded. "Yes. I'm sure."

"Do we have to build a rocket?" asked Atacama.

"No. Objects fall from space all the time. We just need to find a meteorite."

"Star iron," said Innes.

"What?"

"Star iron. I've seen a lump of it. I went on a school trip to that musty old stately home in the hills, Ballindreich. They have a cabinet of curiosities that contains a lump of star iron. My teacher said it landed in the Arctic centuries ago and the local tribes worshipped it, then an explorer claimed it in the name of Empire and brought it back to his fancy house. It's on a shelf, in a wee room, at the top of a tower, just over the moors from here."

"And you want to *steal* it?" asked Beth.

"If you're not coming, you can't criticise."

Molly said, "No, it's a fair point. You really think we should steal it?"

"It's already stolen property. Lord What's-His-Face stole it from an Inuit tribe a couple of hundred years ago.

We could use it to save the world, then post it back to the Arctic."

Molly nodded. "Let's go to Ballindreich."

Beth said, "This is a mistake."

Molly looked up at her. "It might be a mistake, but we can't know until we try. And I already know that sitting about doing nothing would be a much worse mistake. So, who's coming to steal a meteorite?"

As they walked away from Beth again, Innes asked Atacama, "Did you know she was there?"

The sphinx nodded. "I hoped when she heard what we'd seen at the Hall, she'd join us again."

"Not likely," said Innes. "She becomes more tree-centred every time we face a minor problem."

"The Promise Keeper warping the curse arc is hardly a minor problem," said Theo as they crossed the empty field. "We must head straight for Ballindreich."

"We won't get in this late," said Innes. "It's open to the public again in the morning."

Molly said, "You think we should go in the front door, as visitors, when we're planning to remove one of their exhibits?"

"Yeah. It's a dusty old place, and there's only one member of staff, who usually stays at the door selling tickets. We don't need to break into the building, just the cabinet.

Let's meet in the Ballindreich car park at nine o'clock."

"Excellent plan," said Atacama. "It gives me time to do my night shift."

Innes grinned. "Off you trot to your sweetie shop then."

His friends watched as the sphinx ran towards the dark edge of the field.

Then Molly glanced back at the birches, shining silver in the evening light. She couldn't see Beth in the branches any more.

"Will Beth ever come out of her trees again?" asked Molly.

"She's a dryad," said Innes. "She's always much happier in the woods than out of them."

Theo said, "But she has to leave the trees sometimes to do her job properly: to guard trees from the moving world outside their own static sphere. Like kelpies caring for rivers: you have to leave the riverbed and deal with threats from further afield."

Innes snorted. "My dad brings threats *to* his rivers, by breaking rules designed to keep them safe—"

"Don't panic," said a voice behind them.

They all whirled round.

Atacama was crouched on the grass.

"Don't panic," he whispered. "But on my way to work, I crossed a recent scent. And this time I remembered who it was: it's your father, Innes. He's here, watching us, right now."

Chapter Twelve

Molly heard Innes's breathing stutter. She reached out and grabbed his hand. "It's ok. Your dad won't attack you when we're all here."

"But he must be stalking me, waiting until I'm alone, or with a smaller group. He's a hunter. He waits for his chance, then he pounces. He's not going to stop. I'll never be safe."

Innes let out a slow breath. He pulled away from Molly and looked round the dark field. "If I don't face him now, I'll always be scared." He called out, "Dad? I know you're there. Stop skulking in the shadows. Come on out."

The evening air was still and silent.

"Are you afraid? Are you shy? Have you dozed off? Come on, hunter, come and face me!"

The fence at the far edge of the field creaked.

They all turned round and saw Mr Milne walk towards them.

Innes said to his friends, "Stay back. This is between him and me." And he took two paces forward.

Theo said, "Please don't fight your father. Whoever wins, you'll wreck your family. You should work this out with words, not hooves. Are you listening to me, Innes?"

"I hear you. But he's looking for a fight."

As Mr Milne got closer, Molly saw that his face wasn't bleeding any more: it was crisscrossed with long drying wounds. He wasn't limping any more either.

Innes took half a step backwards, then steadied himself. "Were you waiting to catch me on my own?"

"Yes, obviously. That's how a hunter catches his prey. But you're never on your own. You're always with your pet cat, your pet toad, your pet bunny, and now this wingless bird too. I might pick them off one by one. Starting with the weakest, the one at the back of the herd. I might bring down all your friends until there's just you left, my darling son."

"Don't threaten my friends. I know you're angry with me, but don't take it out on them."

"Then let's sort this out one on one, man to man, horse to horse..."

"Fish to fish?" said Innes. "That would be a short fight, in a field. But I don't want to fight you, Dad. You know that's not a solution. Let's both apologise, and both make sure it doesn't happen again. That's what you suggested when Firth let those piranhas loose in the Fiddich. And when Kyle cracked a bridge over the Dullan Water, you said 'We're family, we can forgive each other'. So let's—"

"How can I forgive you? You cursed me. And when you lifted the curse, you left me scarred! I couldn't find the witch Sharpe, so I went to that hedge-witch below the Ben, but she didn't have strong enough herbs to heal me completely. She says I'll have a scarred body forever. My mind is scarred too. All that time as a rock, feeling myself crumble under the water. I still feel the cracks running through me, like loathsome snakes under my skin..." Molly could see his fingers shaking. "You've lifted the curse, but I still feel cursed."

"I'm sorry." Innes walked over to his father and touched his arm. "I wouldn't have cursed you if I'd known the curse would be charged up, that you wouldn't be safe under the water. I just wanted to protect everyone: your prey, but also your family and your rivers from revenge attacks. I thought I was doing the right thing. I really am sorry."

His father pushed him away. "I don't want sympathy or apologies. I want you to suffer the way I've suffered."

"I've got an idea, Dad. I've been too scared to admit to Mum where you've been and what I did to you. But if we tell her together, she'll help us work this out. Let's go home now and—"

"How can I face your mother with these scars? How can I swim my rivers with missing scales and twisted tentacles? You have ruined me! Now I will ruin you..."

The tall kelpie raised his arms. "Innes Milne, I curse—"

Innes yelled, "NO!" and the yell turned into a horse's scream, as Innes reared up and kicked out at his father.

His father's voice stretched and deepened as he shifted into a stallion too.

Atacama yelled, "Get out of their way!"

Molly, Theo, Snib and Atacama stumbled backwards to the fence, as the two horses barged and bit each other, charged and kicked each other, in the middle of the field.

The grey stallion was covered in old wounds, and Innes was adding new wounds with his hooves. Innes was already bleeding too, from cuts on his shoulders.

"How much damage can they do to each other in their horse forms?" asked Molly. "I mean, horses are grass-eating herbivores…"

"There was a sport called horse-fighting in the Philippines," said Theo distantly, as if he was reading from a book, "where, for the crowd's entertainment, stallions fought to the death."

They watched as the horses chased and screamed and battled.

Molly had always been aware of Innes's size and strength as a horse, but he looked like a delicate white pony against his father's massive dappled bulk.

"Can we stop them?" she asked.

Atacama said, "We'd be killed by those hooves if we tried."

"Theo, can't you use your fancy magic?" said Snib. "Can't you wrap them in rainbows or something?"

Theo looked at her blankly, then said, "Not appropriate against a friend or his family. We'll have to think of another way."

They watched the two huge heavy animals attack each other with their weight and speed, their hooves and teeth.

Innes rose up high on his back legs and fell down with both front hooves on his father's head. Mr Milne ducked low and bit at Innes's exposed belly. They were both grunting and screaming.

Molly listened to the noises nervously, even though she knew that horses don't eat meat, so horse sounds shouldn't make her shift shape.

But perhaps shapeshifting was the answer. She asked, "What would shift them back to human, back to a size we can restrain?"

"If we change them to human, Mr Milne will finish casting that curse on Innes," said Atacama.

"Not if we shove my cloak in his mouth," said Theo. "Molly's right, we should shift them back. What can shift a kelpie against their will?"

"Shock," said Atacama. "A sudden shock sometimes shifts Innes to a different shape. It happened when his brother died."

Molly nodded. "When his river turned to salt, he shifted into all his possible shapes while he was trying to escape."

Atacama said, "So we need something that will give Mr Milne a sudden fright."

"Snakes," said Theo. "Horses react instantly to snakes. They rear up, they throw their riders, even if the snakes are harmless."

"Mr Milne definitely doesn't like snakes," said Molly.

"Remember what he said about loathsome snakes under his skin. A snake in the grass might work."

"But where will we get a snake?" asked Snib.

Theo and Atacama both turned to Molly.

She shook her head. "I can't become a snake. Snakes are predators, not prey."

"Lots of predators hunt snakes," said Theo. "We have birds called snake-eagles back home. But..." They all stared at the crashing, thundering, stomping, slashing fury of hooves. "But only if you want to, Molly. Getting close enough to scare him will be dangerous."

Molly shrugged. "Innes would do it for us."

"Then get close and rise up under his father's head. As soon as Mr Milne changes, the rest of us will overpower him and shut him up, so he can't finish that curse."

Molly asked, "What kind of snake am I going to shift into?"

"One that will find a Scottish winter evening quite cold." Theo closed his eyes, cocked his head as if he was listening, then made a bird's call. A high, piercing call, more like a whistle than the black eagle's yelp Molly had heard earlier that day.

Molly felt the usual flash of heat along her spine, but the heat went on for longer and longer and longer as she fell to the ground and became *all* spine.

She turned away from the bird's call, away from the hooves hammering the ground. Then she remembered why she'd shifted. She turned back, her head swaying from side to side, tasting the chilly air. She had to reach the storm of hooves fast, before the cold air and cold ground drained all her energy.

She moved towards the horses, who were now circling each other in the upper corner of the field.

She moved fast, but in a very unfamiliar way: she wasn't running or jumping, but she wasn't slithering either. It was like she was swimming through the air just above the earth, only touching the ground with the edges of her swiftly curving body.

The kelpies were *huge*. Rearing, kicking, snapping, screaming, just in front of her.

Molly stopped, hidden in the grass, feeling the cold damp ground sucking the heat from her body. She wanted to coil up, conserve energy, wait for the sun to rise.

But when she flicked out her tongue, she could taste blood. Salt and iron and heat. The horses were injuring each other; she had to stop them.

The loudest noise, the most blood, the greatest heat from the largest bulk, was to her left. That's where her target was.

She darted forward, between the smashing hooves.

Molly lifted her head, high, high, high. The front of her long body stood straight up, supported by her long tail on the ground.

She hissed, she bared the fangs she could feel against her cheeks and she lunged forward, aiming to sink her fangs into the dappled leg in front of her. She missed by a millimetre. Unable to stop herself, she rose up to strike again...

She heard a terrified shriek.

The horse above her reared, then shifted. First into a fish, flopping onto the grass, then into a man, sitting up and scrambling away.

Molly saw Atacama leap on the man, and heard Theo yell, "Shut up! Don't say a word!"

Molly moved towards the fence, to change back, to get warm.

Behind her, Mr Milne was grunting and bellowing, trying to get words out.

She heard Innes's voice. "He'll never stop. He'll keep trying to hurt me, to hurt all of you. I think... I think I have to..."

Molly heard fear and panic break in his voice, and she sped under the wire fence. She shifted to a girl as she heard Innes say, "I'm sorry, Dad. But I think the only way is to get rid of you forever. So, I..."

Molly vaulted back over the fence and ran towards Innes.

He was standing over his father, raising his hands, ignoring Theo's yells of "No! No!"

Innes was cursing his father again.

Chapter Thirteen

"I, Innes Milne, curse my father, Fraser Milne—"

Molly crashed into him. She crashed hard and low into Innes's ribcage, knocking him sideways, and they both fell to the ground.

She dug her elbow into his belly to knock the remaining breath out of him and she shoved both hands over his mouth. "NO! Don't say it. Don't do it. You can't curse him. Not after what happened last time."

Innes pushed at her and struggled to get her hands off his face. But Molly forced his head back and his lips shut. Innes jerked and twisted, but she used all her strength and determination to hold him down and keep him silent.

Theo ran over to join her, leaving Atacama crouched on Mr Milne's chest, teeth very close to the kelpie's scarred human face.

Theo stood over Innes. "I know a curse seems like a solution. I've used them myself to solve problems like your father. A well-worded curse is a useful piece of magic. But not now, Innes, because no curse is safe, any curse could be charged up. Whatever you do to him, Estelle could make it a hundred times worse."

Innes stopped pushing at Molly and nodded slowly.

She looked at him. "Can we trust you not to do anything stupid? Can we trust you not to say anything you'll regret?"

He nodded, firmly. She pulled her hands away.

He gulped in a deep breath and stood up. "I wasn't going to hurt him. I was going to banish him. I didn't think that was risky. But you're right, no curse is safe."

"Can we trust *you*?" Snib asked Mr Milne. "Can we let you up, without you cursing anyone?"

Mr Milne nodded. Atacama jumped off his chest. The kelpie hauled himself up.

Theo said, "Molly, are you ready to be a snake again?"

Molly moved towards Mr Milne, who flinched and stepped back. She smiled at him, showing her teeth. "Sssso," she drew out the word, "sssso, will the two of you shake hands, and promise not to hunt each other or curse each other again?"

Innes said, "Yes, of course." He stepped forward and held out his hand. "Dad, please. We can't keep this up forever."

"I can. You might not have the stamina for a long vendetta, but I'm a hunter and I can wait. First I'll regain my full strength with creatures who understand vengeance. I hear there's a gathering of those who feed on curses, so I might join them. Then once I have the strength to beat you in a fair fight, boy, I'll hunt you down. I'll stamp on all your little friends too!" He looked at Molly and thumped his foot on the ground, grinding his heel into the earth.

She smiled politely.

Mr Milne turned away and limped across the field.

Innes collapsed onto the ground and put his head in his hands. "I'll have to watch my back every minute of every day from now on."

"Not yet," said Snib. "He said he was going to regain his strength. He won't come after you for a while."

"That's very trusting of you. It might be a trick. He might attack me again tonight..."

"We have a few tricks of our own," said Theo.

"Yeah, the snake." Innes laughed, hoarsely. "That was quite creepy, Molly, you rising up under our hooves like that. But well timed. What were you? You weren't an adder, you were bigger and brighter."

"I've no idea. Something that wanted to be moving over warmer drier ground. What was I, Theo?"

"I didn't get a clear look at you, so I'm not sure. But if you become a snake again, be careful with your fangs. You were probably extremely venomous."

Molly rubbed her cheeks. "I just struck out to scare him. Could I have killed him?"

"I don't know. Just remember, snakes are more dangerous than hares."

Innes sat up straighter and untucked his shirt to examine the bruises and grazes on his ribs. "I wouldn't want to fight him when he's fit and healthy. I couldn't have held out much longer."

Atacama said, "I'm already late for my shift. Will everyone be alright?"

They nodded.

"Then I'll join you tomorrow for a bit of burglary!" The sphinx ran off.

"I can't go home like this." Innes touched a bruise on his face. "Mum will ask questions... I want to bring Dad home, safe and sane, before I tell her what I've done."

Theo pulled him to his feet. "You often go on quests and get into fights. You don't have to tell her who put that hoofprint on your cheek. Just look a bit embarrassed about it and she'll assume you were doing something foolish, but she'll never guess how foolish. Come on."

Molly said, "I'll come too. If snakes are what scare Mr Milne, I should walk Innes home."

They crossed the field and walked through the quiet town to the riverbank where a grey mill-house leant over the water.

"Do you want to sleep in our spare bed, Theo, rather than go back to your cold empty library?" asked Innes. "I can lend you something more sensible than sandals for a journey to Ballindreich tomorrow as well."

"Thanks." Theo smiled. "If I look embarrassed about your bruises too, your mum can assume we've been leading each other astray and battling random monsters all day."

Innes grinned and turned to Molly. "Dad won't be able to catch me on open ground, in daylight, with his injuries. So we'll meet you at Ballindreich tomorrow."

He tidied up his clothes and hair. Then he said, "Thanks for stopping the fight. For shutting my dad up. For shutting me up." He nodded at Snib. "Thanks for preventing us hatching out more crows with more stupid curses. That can't have been easy for you."

Snib frowned. "It might be better if my un-hatched brothers and sisters never leave their eggs. Less pain, less fear, for everyone."

The two girls watched Innes and Theo walk into the mill-house. Snib was standing with her arms wrapped round herself, looking cold and somehow a bit wet, even though it hadn't rained for hours.

Molly sighed. "Where are you going to sleep?"

"I can't go back to Stone Egg Wood, because Corbie will demand to know what you've been talking about. I'll just find a wall to sleep behind, or something." She shivered.

"Don't be daft. Come home with me. I'm sure Aunt Doreen won't mind."

Aunt Doreen didn't mind. She made a larger pan of pasta, and gave the girls a blow-up mattress and duvet to make an extra bed in Molly's tiny room.

"So, Snib," Doreen said, as she sliced more bread, "where do your family live?"

"Out in the moors, towards the mountains," said Snib.

"Do they farm there?"

"My big brother runs a sort of security business, which I think he's trying to expand."

Molly changed the subject, asking Doreen about her chickens' constant bickering and unsuccessful egg-hiding. After bowls of rhubarb crumble, the girls went upstairs to make Snib's bed.

As they lay in the dim room, looking through the skylight at stars being hidden and revealed by invisible clouds, Molly asked, "Did you hear what Mrs Sharpe said?"

"No," said Snib drowsily. "What? When?"

"When she dropped the popcorn, she said to me: 'Ask the crow about the box.' So do you know anything about a box?"

Snib sat up. "I don't know about any boxes. Everyone in Stone Egg Wood keeps their possessions in nests, not boxes."

"What box could Mrs Sharpe have meant?"

"Maybe she didn't say 'crow'. Maybe she said 'Joe' or 'snow' or 'toe'—"

"It was definitely 'crow' and I was right beside you when she said it, so I'm sure she meant you."

"Let me think… A box…?" Snib frowned. "No, no idea." She rubbed her right arm and lay back down.

Molly decided not to press Snib. Either the crow-girl didn't know, or she wasn't going to say. Instead, Molly asked, "What's it like, living in Stone Egg Wood?"

"Noisy! All those baby birds! And sad too, because

so many of us die young. Lots of curses only last a couple of days, or less. And it's been even sadder since so many of us lost our wings. Imagine being able to soar and somersault in the air, then having that torn away from you. To be earthbound when you've owned the sky! I almost wish I'd never flown at all."

Molly nodded. "I know. If I can force Mr Crottel to lift my curse, then I'll never run at hare-speed again. And I will miss it. But I can't wish I'd never become a hare, because at least I'll have memories of speed and strength and beating Innes. And of how much better it is being a hare than a worm or a mouse. But I'll keep turning into worms and mice unless I can find Mr Crottel, and that's not going to be easy, now we know he can turn into a huge green dog as well as a grumpy old witch."

"Your caster is a deephound?" asked Snib. "A big shaggy green hound?"

"Yes, he changed into one this afternoon to chase me."

"Then I might know where he is! When I was leaving Stone Egg Wood to spy on you, a deephound was scratching at the doors. Perhaps he asked Corbie for sanctuary—" Snib gasped. "Oh, I shouldn't have told you that. Now you'll go to Stone Egg Wood tomorrow instead of the big house, and Theo will use his power to force the hound to lift your curse, then..." she put her hands over her eyes, "then my wee brother Mickle will fall."

"Don't worry about that tonight," said Molly. "My first priority is weakening Estelle, to help the other victims.

So I promise I won't tell anyone where Mr Crottel is until we've found that star iron."

Snib smiled at her. "Thank you! So Mickle is safe for another day!" She sighed. "But I wish there was a way to break the link between curses and curse-hatched. Then I could genuinely want you to lose your curse, because your safety wouldn't mean Mickle's death..."

Snib started to sniffle. Molly leant down and patted her shoulder, but the crow-girl rolled away and hid her face under the duvet.

Molly lay back, stared up at the dark ceiling, and wondered if Beth was right about her after all. Had she made that promise to Snib because she didn't want to upset her, because she genuinely wanted to help other curse victims, or because – like Beth kept saying – she wasn't really prepared to do everything possible to lift her own curse?

Snib was breathing calmly now. But Molly took a long time to go to sleep.

"I'm not good with wheels," said Snib, early the next morning, as Molly pulled her own bike and her aunt's bike from the shed. "I'm used to wings."

But Snib stopped wobbling after the first mile, so they cycled fast enough to reach Ballindreich House just before nine o'clock. They pedalled along a frosty avenue of trees shaped oddly like lollipops, then into a car park surrounded by a tall fence formed of trees bent and linked together into uncomfortable-looking curves.

The big house looming over the car park had lots of pale-grey stone carvings and one tall round tower. Just behind it was a ruined castle, with tumbledown walls and broken staircases.

They put their bikes in the bike shelter, which was much fancier than the one in Aberrothie. It had a gilded clan crest on the brusque sign saying:

Bikes are left
at owners risk

Molly glanced at the floor to see if the apostrophe had fallen off, then she heard hoofbeats.

Innes and Theo were approaching across a field, from a line of trees that looked more natural than the trees near the house. Theo slipped off Innes's back, and Innes hid behind the bike shelter while he shifted.

Atacama appeared from the trees just as a yellow car drove into a space marked:

Staff Only

The sphinx slid along the ground behind the bike shelter, while a tall lady in green tartan locked the car, then unlocked the huge carved door to the house. "We don't open until half past nine," she yelled, and slammed the door behind her.

Atacama said, "When she lets you in, I'll wait outside and keep watch."

"Keep your eyes and nostrils open for my dad, please," said Innes, "and for any other dangerous arrivals."

"Who else is likely to be following us?" asked Molly.

Innes shrugged. "Perhaps a little bird has told Corbie what we're doing this morning? If Corbie approves of Estelle charging up curses, he might try to stop us."

Snib stared up at him. "If you mean this little bird, I was with Molly all night. And I'm on your side. If Corbie approves of what the Promise Keeper is doing, he's wrong. I haven't told him anything, honestly."

"I believe her," said Molly. "But you should look out for Mr Milne, Atacama. Though haven't you been up all night?"

"I'm fine," he said. "I'm used to nightshifts."

While they waited for the custodian to open up, they wandered round the outside of the house. Innes led them to the foot of the tower. "The cabinet is in the room at the top. Look, you can see the window."

Theo walked round to the ruined castle and stood under a crested sign saying:

Do not allow children
to play on the stonework.
Ballindreich House
takes no responsibility
for any injuries.

Theo looked at the crumbling walls. "The old house was built right onto this older ruin."

They heard the front door being opened wide on creaky hinges. Molly used her holiday money to pay for four of them to enter at child prices.

The woman in tartan asked, "Do you want the children's treasure maps or the adult guides?"

Innes said, "Treasure maps, please," at the same time as Theo said, "Proper guides, please."

Molly said, "One of each, thank you."

The woman said, "Do you want crayons, to colour in the treasure map?"

Molly shook her head. "Not today, thanks."

The woman shrugged and picked up a magazine.

They walked into the first room, where they squashed into a corner behind a golden rope, and stared from a distance at flowery armchairs and portraits of children on ponies.

They walked along the corridor, peeking into a dining room with dusty plates and four forks per setting, then a library full of leather-bound books, with volume numbers stamped in gold.

Molly wanted to stop and decipher the faint book titles. What subject could possibly need twenty-five volumes?

But Innes said, "Come on, the tower is at the other end."

They walked briskly past all the other rooms.

When they reached the curving stone staircase, they saw something sitting on the bottom step.

A cat.

A pale cat, with dark paws and dark ears. A slim sharp Siamese cat, looking quietly at them.

Snib whispered, "Molly, be very careful."

Innes said, "If your curse is triggered and you shift, run straight to one of us. We'll scoop you up and keep you safe."

The cat opened its mouth.

Molly flinched.

But the cat simply yawned, silently. And started washing its ears, gently and silently.

Innes said, "Let's get past, without disturbing it."

He stepped carefully onto the bottom step.

The cat hissed at him.

Molly changed into a mouse.

And the cat leapt off the step...

Chapter Fourteen

Molly wanted to run away.

She was becoming familiar with her mouse body. Her mouse form was nimble, though not able to move fast enough or jump far enough for her liking, and that tail was just asking to be pounced on. She knew that every tiny bone in her mouse body wanted to run. Away from the suddenly intent cat, away from the dangerously lumbering humans. She wanted to find a small space and hide there, shivering.

But she remembered what Innes had said. Run towards one of them and they'd keep her safe. So she ran, straight towards the cat. Straight towards her friends' tree-trunk legs.

She felt a hand scoop her up. A terrifyingly huge hand, smelling of bike oil, toast, pencil lead and feathers.

Snib's hand.

She heard the cat yowl and Snib yell, "Oy, get down!"

Innes said, "No scratching. Leave her alone!"

Molly was dropped into a small space. She fell on her back, her paws flailing. She righted herself in a warm corner of Snib's cardigan pocket. Tiny holes in the knitting let in enough dim light for her to see a long wooden object, which she had an immediate desire to gnaw. She rolled over onto a crinkly sheet of something less comfy than the soft fabric.

Then the huge hand grabbed her again and pulled her out.

Molly was squirming in Snib's fingers, high above Snib's head.

She heard Innes's voice. "Hey puss. You're not getting the mouse, so stop climbing the crow's legs."

The voice of the custodian echoed up the corridor: "Is everything alright?"

Theo called back, "It's fine. We've just met your cat."

"He won't bother you, so long as you stay behind the ropes."

"And so long as none of us are mice," muttered Innes.

Molly was still in Snib's hand, her tail and body floppy with fright and frustration.

Snib said, "Theo, can't you get rid of this cat? You're the one with all the power..."

Theo said in a distracted tone, "No, if I do any magic, I risk blowing up the whole county. Innes?"

"No space to turn into a horse, and if I become a pike this beast will try to eat me. Snib, I don't suppose you have power over cats?"

"No more than anyone else. But I'll give it a go." Snib passed Molly to Innes, who held her gently cupped in his hands, close to his chest. Molly peeked between his fingers, as Snib bent down, looked the cat in the eyes and hissed.

The cat backed away, then ran up the stairs.

Snib stood up. "I'd better take her again, Innes, your jeans are too tight for her to be safe in your pocket."

Innes handed Molly over.

"Are you ok, Molly-mouse?" Snib smiled at her, a scary tooth-filled grin. "I'll put you in an empty pocket, that'll be comfier."

Molly landed in the empty pocket, slightly annoyed there was nothing to chew on. She was bounced into a woolly corner, as the crow-girl followed the kelpie and the magician up the stairs.

Innes said, "Don't bother with the nursery or the servants' rooms. The cabinet is at the top of the tower."

Molly hoped the cat was hiding from Snib in one of the rooms they walked past, rather than waiting for them at the top.

When they reached the last step, Snib lifted Molly out of her pocket. "So you can see. It's probably not nice hiding in a pocket."

Molly couldn't tell her that mice like hiding in small spaces, and that mice don't like being held in big hot hands out in the open.

But she looked around anyway.

Innes pointed over another golden rope at a glass-fronted cabinet with rows of objects on its shelves. "The cabinet of curiosities!"

Theo read from the guide: "It contains fascinating fossils, genuine geological specimens and real royal relics from Scottish history. Apparently."

Innes read from the treasure map. "Also a hilt from a Portuguese pirate's sword, medals won by families on the Ballindreich estate, a fairy princess's acorn tea-set and a prehistoric shark's tooth. And a stolen meteorite, of course."

Theo stepped over the rope.

Molly saw a sudden predatory movement, so she yelled a warning at the top of her voice, which came out as a pathetic squeak. The Siamese cat leapt at Theo, scratching his knee through his linen trousers.

Theo backed off.

The cat jumped to the top of the cabinet and crouched there, one paw dangling down, claws scraping against the glass door.

Innes laughed and helped Theo back across the rope. "It's a guard cat. Let me try." He climbed over the rope and walked towards the cabinet.

The cat swiped at Innes's face. He ducked.

"How do we get past it?" asked Snib.

Innes said, "Molly-mouse could run round the room to lure the cat away, while I get the star iron."

Theo and Snib both said, "No!"

Innes shrugged. "Ok. Lend me your cloak then, Theo."

Innes wrapped the fabric round his hand and tried to open the glass door. The cat's claws slashed down.

Innes stepped away, looking at the blood seeping through the pale linen. "It's locked. We can't pick the lock with that mini-tiger up there, and if we break the glass the tartan lady downstairs will hear. We need to find the key or get rid of that cat."

The cat slashed again, his tail lashing. Molly saw the tail knock a white shape from the top of the cabinet, which fell to the floor with a crash.

They heard a distant voice: "What are you children doing up there?"

Snib said, "We should leave now and come back later."

Theo nodded. "Innes, get back over the rope."

Snib yelled down, her voice so loud that Molly vibrated in her hand, "Your cat knocked over a coronation mug. We're just coming down—"

The woman's voice boomed up the stairs. "I'm coming up. Stay where you are."

They stood in the middle of the floor, looking guilty; the cat sat on the cabinet, washing his paws and looking innocent.

Snib hid Molly in her pocket as the custodian reached the top of the stairs.

"The cat knocked that mug down with his tail," said Snib. "It was nothing to do with us. We were all behind the rope, all the time, honestly."

The woman scowled. "That cat is a menace, but he belongs to the owner, so I can't get rid of him. I'll sweep it up later. Where's your friend? There were four of you."

Innes said, "She's looking at the nursery. She likes cuddly toys. Especially toy mice…"

"Please leave together. It makes it easier to keep track."

As she stomped down the stairs, Theo muttered, "We'll have to return for the star iron."

"Which stone is the star iron?" asked Snib.

Theo glanced at the guide, then pointed to the top shelf. "That shiny rock there, between the sword hilt and the royal relics."

Innes said, "But—"

Molly heard a thump and Innes said, "Ow. Ok. Yes. That's it. The shiny one on the top shelf. I remember it."

As they walked down the stairs, Snib asked, "What will we do about Molly? That woman expects to see four of us leave."

Innes said, "But Molly can't shift back until we cross the estate boundary."

Theo smiled. "So let's create a boundary here." He stepped into the dining room. "Put Molly on the floor. Snib, keep an eye out for the cat. Innes, create a boundary around Molly."

"Why me?"

"You created a circle to imprison me last year."

"But it took ages to prepare. Can't you do it, Theo?"

"You know why I can't do it."

"Can't the crow-girl do it?"

"Not since I removed her shape-shifting magic."

"But… I don't want to do it wrong!"

"You won't. I'll be watching."

Innes ducked under the rope and lifted a sugar bowl off the dining table, then laid the dusty round-edged sugar cubes in a careful circle round Molly, who was desperate to sneak forward and nibble one.

As he held the last cube above the wooden floor, Molly saw Innes frown and take a deep breath. He laid the sugar down and she felt a chill in the air. He'd made a boundary.

Molly dashed forward, resisted the temptation to gnaw the sugar, and leapt the boundary.

She crashed into Innes and Theo, her sudden human weight knocking them both onto the floor with a clatter and a thud.

"*What are you doing now?*" yelled the woman. "You'd better leave, before you break anything else!"

Innes scooped up the sugar cubes, dropped them in the bowl and put it on the table, then all four of them walked along the corridor to the front desk.

"That was very interesting," Molly said to the woman in tartan. "Thanks so much."

Then she noticed a rack of keys on hooks, behind the woman's head. She nudged Innes and pointed to the rack, then she smiled at the custodian. "Can you answer a few questions for me? What colour was the pirate's beard, and how did he break his sword? Do fairies drink herbal tea or ordinary tea from their acorn teacups? And does the twenty-five-volume story in the library have a 'happy ever after' ending?"

While the tartan-clad woman was trying to answer Molly's quick-fire questions, Innes slipped behind the desk and grabbed a key.

Molly asked one more question: "Is your cat any good at catching mice? Because we think a mouse has been nibbling the sugar cubes in the dining room, so maybe the cat isn't doing his job properly?"

Innes walked out the door. "Come on. Stop annoying the nice lady with silly questions."

"Sorry!" Molly ran out of Ballindreich House and caught up with the other three, as they walked across the car park.

"Thanks for saving me from the cat, and for making a boundary."

"I should teach *you* how to make a boundary," said Theo, "then you can choose where and when you shift back to human."

"Could you? Could I? But I'm not magic."

"Yes, you are. You're currently filled with so much curse magic and shapeshifting magic, you could make an effective boundary circle the size of Wales."

They'd left Atacama in the shadows behind the bike shelter, and that's where they found him – curled up, black cat's tail round black human nose – snoozing in the grass.

Innes said, "So much for keeping watch."

A familiar voice said, "I kept a lookout."

Beth stepped round the side of the shelter and over the gently snoring sphinx. "But now I see that you took

133

a dark dangerous curse-hatched into the house with you. I certainly haven't seen anything darker or more dangerous than her this morning."

"What are you doing here?" asked Innes. "I thought you were staying with your trees."

She sighed. "They torture the trees on this estate. I'm here to do some gentle healing."

She walked over to the trees that were bent and wound together like a giant's toast rack at the edge of the car park. She laid her hand on the nearest trunk. "They're so domesticated they don't have their own dryads, so I visit sometimes. I can't change the way they're forced to grow, but I can remind them that they're trees, not ornaments. If you're doing something that will annoy the tree-torturing owners here, I might help you."

"We're going to steal a rock from them tonight," said Molly.

"Is it in there?" Beth looked up at the tower.

"On the top shelf of the cabinet at the top of the tower," said Theo. "It's the glitteriest rock in there, it won't be hard to spot."

"We don't have to wait until tonight," said Innes. "I checked the opening times. In the quiet season, before Easter, they close at noon. If we wait a couple of hours, the tartan lady will go home."

"What about the cat?" asked Molly.

"There's no need to be scared of the cat," said Theo, "if I can teach you to make a boundary."

"You can't teach Molly magic!" said Beth. "She's not a witch—"

Atacama snuffled, stretched and looked up. "Oh, there you all are." He yawned. "I just... closed my eyes for a minute..."

Innes smiled. "You fell asleep on duty, sphinx. Perhaps you need a cat nap before we break into the house."

"Didn't you get the star iron? Do you need to break in?" Atacama stood up and flexed his claws. "I'll join you this time. I've always thought I'd be a wonderful cat burglar."

Theo said, "If I'm going to teach Molly how to create magical boundaries, I'll need somewhere with flat earth or gravel, but not as public as this car park."

"There are clear flat spaces in the walled garden to the east of the house," said Innes. "Let's go there, if everyone is awake."

Molly looked round for Snib, who'd been very quiet since Beth called her dark and dangerous. Snib was stretching up to the roof of the bike shelter. She saw Molly looking at her, and smiled. "My back's a bit stiff after that blow-up mattress. Just getting the kinks out."

Then Molly walked towards the walled garden, to learn her first deliberate magic spell.

Chapter Fifteen

Molly sat cross-legged inside a circle scratched in the grey gravel of a garden filled with sad roses and regimented herbs.

All her friends stood round her: Theo biting his lip and thinking, Innes on the verge of laughter, Beth frowning, Atacama grooming his tail, Snib looking nervously at the sky.

"Do I have to be sitting down? The ground's really cold, and I feel silly."

"Magic is not silly," said Theo. "Magic is serious."

"Magic is dangerous," said Beth.

"Being a mouse chased by a cat is more dangerous," said Innes.

"So she shouldn't be learning magic, she should be searching for Mr Crottel and forcing him to change his mind," said Beth.

Molly glanced at Snib, who shrugged slightly, but didn't say anything.

Molly said, "We don't have time to look for Mr Crottel

now. We have to break into the house in a couple of hours. There's just time for a beginner's guide to magical geometry. Theo, tell me how to make a boundary."

"The principle of a boundary is the dynamic tension between the shape created and the intent of the creator..."

Innes yawned, but Theo continued "...so we need to utilise the perfection of the circle and the motion of—"

Snib interrupted, "She won't have time to draw a perfect circle. You saw her. She was a shivering little mouse. And that cat was fast and vicious."

"I see what you mean... Perhaps we don't need the absolute power of the circle. We can probably use a line." Theo drew a line in the grit with his foot. "A straight line isn't as satisfying as a circle, but it will work. So, Molly, first mark a line. As you draw it, place a tiny bit of magical power into the line, a fragment of the magic inside you. Innes, when you made the sugar cube circle, what did you put in?"

Innes grinned. "I thought about the thunder of my hooves on the earth."

"Excellent. Molly, that's the sort of power to place in the line, a strong feeling or image from your own experience of magic. Then consciously recognise that this side of the line is here and that side is there, so the line separates one place from another. That makes the line into a genuine boundary. Then leap over it. Finally, remember to break the line. Don't leave random magic lying around. Do you understand all that?"

Molly made a face, then nodded.

"So find a clear space."

Molly stood up and walked to a gap between beds of lavender and rosemary.

"Now, draw a line, putting the power of your own personal magic into it."

Molly bent down and drew a line. As she moved her index finger through the grit, she thought of sprinting in a straight line, the wind pushing her hare ears straight back.

Theo said, "That's good. I can feel that. Don't lift your finger yet. Now concentrate on the line, and be aware this side is *here*, that side is *there* and they are very different. Then lift your finger."

Molly looked at the tiny sharp stones at her feet and the tiny sharp stones on the other side of the line. She saw that they were all slightly different and the line separated those differences. She lifted her finger.

Everyone around her sighed.

"Perfect," said Theo.

"Even I felt that," said Innes.

"You're a natural," said Snib.

"She's not a natural," snapped Beth. "She's simply following Theo's precise instructions. And stop talking about her 'own personal magic'. It's not her magic, it's dark magic."

Theo smiled. "We're all a mix of light and dark. Even you, Beth. Even your gentle trees."

Molly stepped away from her first magical line.

"Break it," Theo said. "Always tidy up after yourself when you're doing magic."

Molly rubbed her hand across the middle of the line and felt a sudden slight sadness. She'd broken something perfect.

"Well, that was fascinating," said Innes. "But no use at all."

"What do you mean, no use?" said Theo. "I thought it was rather good, for her first time."

"Yes, but she needs to do it as a hare or a mouse, not a girl."

So Molly shifted into her hare self and held out her right paw. Could she draw a line as a hare?

She touched the ground and swept her paw left to right, but the line was shallow, curved and wobbly, rather than firm and straight. Molly placed her paw on the ground again and backed away, dragging her paw behind her. This time she made a deeper, clearer line.

But she'd forgotten to put anything magical into it. So she broke that line with her tail, ignoring Innes's snort of laughter.

Molly drew another line, thinking about the finish line of a race and how it felt to win as a hare. Then she looked at the grit, on one side and the other, fixing the difference in her mind. Finally she lifted her paw.

She leapt over the line.

And landed on the ground as a girl.

She rolled over and stood up, to a round of applause.

"Wow," said Innes. "That's amazing. You can now shift into a hare and shift into a girl, entirely by your own choice. You've made the curse magic your own, Molly Drummond. Wow."

Molly smiled. And smudged the middle of the line with her heel.

She turned away from her friends and leant against the chilly grey wall of the garden, staring at, but not really seeing, a small pale mushroom growing between two stones.

She could become a hare whenever she wanted, by choosing her hare form; she could become a girl whenever she wanted, by drawing a line. She wondered what else she could do. But first she had to master this boundary magic.

She turned round. "I need animal noises, to see if I can do this when I'm something less familiar than a hare."

Atacama miaowed softly.

Molly became a mouse. She crouched in the shadow of the wall, drew a line with her paw, and thought about the long line of her mouse's tail. She saw the difference between here and there, then lifted her paw. She jumped the line and hit the wall with her shoulder.

"Ouch. Lesson one. Leave myself enough space to shift!"

She rubbed out the tiny line. "What else?"

Innes howled and Molly became a deer. She made a line with her hoof, putting her speed and elegance into it, then leapt over it.

She landed on her hooves. She shook her slim head,

smudged the first line, and made another, putting in her speed as she drew, then remembering to see the ground on either side as here and there. She leapt again and rolled over as a girl.

"Lesson two. Don't rush it."

"But you'll need to rush it," said Innes. "A real wolf would have been chasing you."

"So let's try this spell at speed. Who wants to chase me?"

Atacama grinned. "Me…" And he growled his own low reverberating snarl.

Molly shifted into a goat and galloped to the other side of the garden as Atacama ran towards her. She scraped a line in the earth with magical memories hard in her head, she looked at the ground – one side, the other side – then she lifted her hoof—

And was knocked over by the furry impact of a fast-moving black body.

"Got you," said Atacama.

She nudged him off with her horns and jumped the line.

"Lesson three. Sphinxes are faster than they look. I have to become even faster. I have to create the boundary in fewer steps."

Theo walked over. "You mark the line, placing power into the line, you see *here* and *there*, you lift your paw or hoof. Then you jump."

Molly nodded.

"That's the minimum you can do to make the spell viable."

"But it's too many steps when I'm being chased."

Snib said, "Why not look at the two sides of the line as you draw it? See here and there as you separate them?"

Theo nodded. "That might work. Try it."

Molly looked at Beth. "Could you hoot like an owl?"

Beth folded her arms and shook her head.

Snib said, "I'll do an eagle. I've heard lots of raptors at home recently."

She called, high and piercing, and Molly shifted into something oddly familiar but also completely different. Like a hare, but smaller, weaker and considerably less sure of herself.

"A rabbit!" Innes laughed. "Let's make this realistic. Let's *all* chase her."

Every single one of Molly's friends took a threatening step towards her.

Innes said, "Everything eats rabbits. Everything likes a bit of rabbit stew. So imagine that Snib's an eagle, I'm a fox, Beth's a stoat, Atacama's a lion, Theo's a rabbit-eating toad and we're all coming to get you..."

Molly drew a line, fast, with magic powering into it, and a here on one side and a there on the other, then lifted her paw, leapt, and crashed into a rose-bush with her human hip.

"That's fast," said Theo. "Really fast. Well done! You need to practise though, to be sure you're safe."

"You can never be sure you're safe," said Beth. "Because not every prey animal can draw a line."

The dryad trilled a fragment of birdsong.

Molly became a worm.

A worm, with no hooves or paws.

Though Molly couldn't quite remember what she'd have done with paws...

Then she saw a shadow above her.

She burrowed into the loose earth of the flower bed, and as she burrowed, she recalled that straight lines were important, for some reason, so she burrowed in a straight line, just under the surface, focussing as hard as she could in her boneless body on straight and line and line and straight, and earth to one side, and different earth to the other, then she pushed up towards the air.

She squirmed out into the light, and wriggled round to cross the line from above, though she was a bit fuzzy about why that was necessary.

Before she crossed the line, Molly felt a pincer-grip round her soft body and was lifted into the air.

Beth held Molly above her open mouth. As she dangled, Molly could feel the dryad's warm breath.

"You're dead," Beth said. "The bird caught you."

She lowered Molly, then moved her gently across the underground line. And Molly was human again, curled up under the rose bush.

Beth held out her hand and helped Molly up.

"Theo's fancy spells won't keep you alive if a real predator is chasing you. You can't rely on your speed to save you, because something will eventually be faster than you. You can't rely on your friends to save you, because we won't always be there. And you can't rely on magic to save you, because it's magic that's endangering you. You *must* lift your curse."

"But I don't think I can." Molly looked round at everyone. "If I break or lift my curse, a bird will die. He's Snib's little brother and he's called Mickle. I don't think I can take a decision that will kill a curse-hatched. Especially not now I have ways to keep myself safe. Not completely safe, but safer than I was yesterday."

Beth squeezed her hand. "Molly! You can't put the life of a curse-hatched bird over your own life."

Molly glanced at Snib. "I think I have to. I think sacrificing someone I've never even properly met, in order to save myself, is a much darker use of magic than any spells we've been playing with today."

She looked away from Snib's surprised face and Beth's shocked one, and saw birds swooping up from the car park towards to the clouds. "Have those birds been spying on us? Are they crows?"

But the three birds were already too far away for her to be sure.

Chapter Sixteen

As they hid in the narrow lunchtime shadows and watched the Ballindreich House custodian lock the front door, Molly asked quietly, "What are we taking Rosalind as a birthday present?"

Beth said, "I carved a wooden pendant weeks ago."

"My brother is taking her a bottle of fancy bubble bath," said Innes.

Atacama smiled. "My wee sisters are giving her a fluffy blanket. They're all very excited about how cuddly it is."

"We have to take her something together," said Molly. "Or at least Theo, Snib and I do..."

"But I haven't been invited," murmured Snib.

"True," said Beth. "So you don't need to worry about a present."

Molly sighed. "We don't exactly have time to go shopping."

"Just come without a present," said Beth. "Rosalind won't mind."

There was a moment's silence, while they all considered the truth of that statement.

Beth laughed. "Ok, she will mind, but she'll get over it, once we cut the cake."

They watched the custodian drive off in her yellow car, then Innes said, "Time to liberate a lump of star iron." He pulled a key out of his back pocket, and pointed to the cream label hanging off it:

Cab. of Curio.

"What about the front door?" asked Atacama.

"The front door key wasn't on the rack. We'll have to break in."

They walked round the house, looking for a way in. But every window was locked and every door was bolted. The courtyard of the ruined castle was easy to get into, but there were no doors from the ancient building to the old one.

They returned to the heavy front door and looked at the small diamond-paned windows either side of it.

Innes said, "I could kick the glass in."

Molly said, "I know it's not stealing to take the star iron, because they stole it from northern tribes, but I'm not sure about damaging—"

A small stone hit the ground in front of her.

She jumped back. Another stone bounced painfully off her shoulder. More stones clattered on the steps beside her.

She linked her hands over her head to protect her face and looked up. Above her, three small grey figures were perched on the gutter, chucking stones down.

"What are they?" asked Molly.

"Fungus fairies," said Beth. "They work with us in the woods, decomposing and recycling." Molly realised she'd seen them rooting in the earth the day before. They were three or four times the height of flower fairies, and much bulkier.

Beth yelled up, "Manky, Minging and Mawkit? What are you doing up there?"

The largest of the figures on the roof called back, "Hello, Beth. What are *you* doing down there? You seem to be choosing the wrong side. We've chosen the right side."

"What side, Manky? What do you mean?"

"Corbie and his curse-hatched are building a curse-empowered army. And we're joining them."

"The curse-hatched aren't building an army!" Beth looked round. "Are they?"

Theo shrugged. "They're still afraid of my power. At least, they were..."

Manky waved a glittery object. "This is proof of our loyalty to Corbie. We'll present it to him soon." He glanced up at the clouds.

"Are they on their way, Manky?" asked the shortest fairy.

"Be patient, Minging."

"Is that the star iron?" asked Molly. "I didn't see it properly when I was a mouse."

Snib said, "Yes, that's the star iron he's holding, isn't it?"

Theo and Innes looked at each other and nodded.

"We have to get it from them," said Molly, "before whatever they're waiting for arrives."

"Crows," muttered Beth. "That's what they're waiting for, the daft mushrooms. Perhaps I can talk some sense into them." She called up again. "You're not curse-casters or curse-hatched. Why do you want to work with Corbie?"

"Because fungus thrives on darkness, death and decay, on everything curses leave behind them," replied Manky. "If we join Corbie's curse army, our fungi will grow on juicier food than fallen trees in your little grey wood." His squelching laugh was clear four stories below.

"They're not going to see sense." Innes frowned at Theo. "We have to try to stop them, don't we?"

Theo nodded.

"Just *try* to stop them?" said Molly. "Let's aim higher than that, and actually succeed."

"How can we stop them?" asked Beth.

Molly said, "I thought you weren't getting involved. I thought you were staying with your trees."

Beth shrugged. "If Corbie's building a curse army, we all have to take sides. And if he's poaching my wood's fungus fairies, I'm already involved."

"Let's get to the roof and grab that rock before their feathery taxi arrives," said Molly.

"How can we reach the roof?" asked Snib. "We don't have a key to get in."

"We don't need to climb up the inside," said Innes. "We can climb up the outside." He ran to the castle courtyard, to the ruins that led right up to the roof of the house. "Race you all to the top!"

"Not everything is a race," said Beth.

Innes laughed and started to climb the wall nearest the tower.

Molly didn't rush to follow him. She looked at the tumbledown walls. Would it be useful to shift to her hare self?

The ruined walls weren't smooth and flat. There were steps, ledges and arches, so perhaps the ability to leap from one stone to another would be helpful. She could see a route where she could get more than halfway up in a series of jumps. But eventually, she'd have to climb straight up, which wouldn't be possible without fingers. And the narrow top of a wall wouldn't be a safe place to create a boundary and shift back to human.

So she should climb as a girl.

She ran to the wall that Innes and Snib were already scrambling up, but started further from the tower. She didn't want to get caught in a vertical traffic jam.

Atacama chose the route Molly had considered as a hare. He leapt from stone to stone, flapping his tiny wings and swishing his long tail for balance.

Beth and Theo were climbing a route on a different wall.

Molly knew that, unlike the climbing walls in her local sports centre, these handholds and footholds weren't guaranteed safe, so she tested each one before putting her weight on it.

She took a break on the sill of a high window and looked round.

Atacama was already higher than her, but he'd run out of ledges and steps. He was stretching up the featureless wall above him, but he couldn't find anywhere to put his front paws.

The blobby grey fungus fairies had moved along the roof of Ballindreich House to stand above the castle walls. They were amusing themselves by waggling their bottoms and kicking small pebbles down.

The loudest and tallest of them, Manky, was waving the star iron and shouting insults at Innes. The smallest one, Minging, was dancing above Atacama and shouting, "Here kitty kitty, here kitty kitty!" The third fairy, the plumpest and squashiest, was dropping gravel and making farty noises above Molly.

She ignored him and kept climbing, searching for jutting corners of grey stone and trying not to think about the hard landing below her.

She was halfway up. To her left, Snib and Innes were climbing steadily too.

But on the wall to her right, Beth and Theo had stopped. Theo shouted across, "We can't see any more reliable handholds. We're going down."

Molly could see Atacama leaping from one ledge to another at the same height, searching for any route that would get him to the top. He shouted, "I can't get higher either. Sorry."

Molly stretched up to the next handhold, and the fairy above her squealed, "I've run out of pebbles. And this long bony person is getting too close to me."

"If you're scared, Mawkit, walk round to me," said Manky. "They won't catch us, don't worry."

"Won't we?" shouted Innes. "You can see us getting closer. Can you see your crow friends yet? Maybe you should worry, fungus-face! Maybe you should just drop the star iron now, then we'll climb down and leave you alone."

"Don't be rude to them," called Beth as she reached the ground.

"Why not? They've been waggling their bottoms at us."

Theo shouted, "Innes, Molly, Snib. We've tried to rescue the star iron, that's the important thing. Don't put yourself at risk, it's not worth it."

Molly yelled, "Yes, it is worth it, for all those curse victims!"

The three fungus fairies gathered in a pale grey huddle on the roof. Molly heard them whispering and chanting.

Molly wondered if she could beat Innes at vertical races as well as horizontal ones. She glanced over, to see if he was ahead of her.

And her left hand slipped off the stone.

"Concentrate," she muttered. "It's not really a race."

She put her hand back on the stone and it slipped again. Molly realised the stone didn't feel gritty. It felt smooth and fleshy.

Then she felt something moving under her right hand, and saw little white shapes growing between her fingers. Molly reached up for a new hold, but the stone edge broke off in her hand and crumbled into soft lumps.

It wasn't stone; it was mushroom.

The wall above her was sprouting mushrooms and toadstools.

"Careful!" yelled Innes. "It's growing really fast."

The whole wall was covered in fungi growing as speedily as time-lapse photography on a nature programme. Molly couldn't see any safe holds.

Beth shouted from below, "Knock the growths off, then grab the stone underneath before more can grow."

Molly looked up. She couldn't see any grey stone, just smooth domes of creamy white and nut brown and bright yellow.

Molly stretched up and scraped a patch of wall clear of fungi. She looked for handholds past the instant regrowth of new caps, and when she saw jutting stone, she grabbed at it and held on tight, despite the fungi pushing against her fingers. She kicked at the mushrooms round her feet until she found footholds. And she kept climbing up.

Innes and Snib were still climbing too, helping each other clear space and spot handholds.

She heard Beth below, calling out instructions: "Molly, there are good holds to your left, about forty-five degrees from—"

Her voice stopped suddenly. Molly glanced down.

Theo was whispering to Beth.

Then Beth yelled up, "It's not safe! Molly, Innes, it looks really dangerous from here. Come down *now*!"

"What do you think, Molly?" asked Innes.

"I'm going up, not down."

So they kept climbing the fungus-covered wall.

Molly could feel the fungi pushing out from the stone, all down her body, trying to knock her off the wall. But she kept swiping at the spongy growths above her, flicking tiny toadstools away with her fingertips.

Snib called over, "Careful, I think some of them are poisonous."

"Don't worry. I'm not going to stop for a snack." Molly dug her fingers into a cold crevice and moved up a few more centimetres.

Then she heard Snib say, "Watch out Innes, that's not—"

She heard Innes say, "Ooops, that wasn't—"

Molly turned round to see Innes holding on with just one hand, the other hand and both feet flailing.

He hung for a moment, then he fell.

The kelpie yelled in anger and shock, then landed in a nasty heap on the top step of a broken staircase.

"Are you ok?" called Molly.

"Ouch! That was extremely... ouch. Careful, both of you. Some of those mushrooms are the same colour as the stonework. If you can't get up safely, leave those nasty slimy fairies with their stupid shiny rock and come down."

Snib and Molly looked at each other. They were at almost the same height, with an expanse of fungus-covered wall between them and a whole ruined castle below.

"Do you want to keep climbing?" asked Molly.

"Absolutely!" said Snib. "You?"

Molly nodded. "See you at the top."

"They're not stopping, Manky," called Mawkit. "They're unstoppable monster things..."

Molly grinned. She was about ten times as tall as the fungus fairies. Perhaps she did seem like a monster to them. She broke off more fungi and grasped another corner of stone.

"They're not monsters. They're just children. We're the powerful ones," yelled Manky. "Are you ready, Minging?"

Then something sneezed at Molly. One of the fast-growing fungi sneezed a puff of smoky dust in her face. Molly jerked her head away, jerking her hand off the wall at the same time.

She flailed and grabbed, and as her hand found a grip, her right foot slipped off. But she held steady with both hands until her foot found a secure space again. She yelled, "Beth, what's that smoky stuff?"

"Spores. Sort of like mushrooms' seeds. Don't breathe them in. Please come down, Molly."

Molly coughed and kept going.

Then Snib was surrounded by a cloud of spores, and she speeded up to climb out into clear air.

Molly shouted, "Careful! Don't rush!"

"But I can't see..." Snib's foot slipped and her hand snatched at the air.

There was nothing Molly could do, as she watched the crow-girl fall back from the wall and tumble through the air.

She didn't land on a step, like Innes, she fell all the way to the courtyard.

"Snib!" yelled Molly.

Snib didn't answer.

Molly saw Atacama and Theo sprint to the grey heap on the ground.

"Is she ok?"

Theo shouted, "I don't know yet. It's too dangerous, Molly. Come down."

Molly looked at Snib crumpled on the ground. She looked at the fungus fairies grinning at her from the top of the wall. She saw the star iron glittering in Manky's fist.

She kept climbing.

Then she heard Minging mutter again.

Suddenly, the fungi started to sag and slide into liquid around her fingers.

The hat-shaped mushroom in front of her nose turned black, and she could feel the wall oozing, and her feet and hands slipping. The fungi were decaying faster than ice melting in a hot drink. The wall was covered in soupy rotting gunk.

She tried to grasp the handholds above her. She could

see them more easily now, as the fungi rotted and slid down the stones. But she couldn't grasp them. Her fingers were slick with slime.

She jammed her left hand into a crevice and tried to pull herself up.

Her fingers slid out.

Her left foot slipped.

Her right hand slithered down the wall.

Molly knew she was going to fall a second before it happened. But she was as powerless to help herself as she had been to help Innes or Snib.

She started to slide downwards. She grabbed a handhold she'd already used, but her weight and speed wrenched her fingers off.

Now Molly wasn't holding onto anything.

All she could do was fall.

Chapter Seventeen

Molly landed hard on the high window sill.

Her breath was knocked from her chest and her teeth rattled in her jaws, but she managed to grab the gritty edge of the stone ledge with her slimy hands, to stop herself tumbling and falling the rest of the way.

She looked up. The wall above her was dripping with decay.

The fairies higher up were giggling.

Even higher, six black shapes were swooping towards the fairies.

Molly watched the three pairs of crows stretch out their claws and pick up the three fungus fairies.

Then the crows carried Manky, Minging, Mawkit and the star iron into the clouds.

By the time Molly stumbled to the ground and wiped her stinking hands on the grass, Snib was sitting up between Atacama and Theo, cradling her left arm against her chest.

Her face was paler than ever, and her nose and cheekbones looked even sharper. But she was conscious and she was talking.

Or at least, she was listening while Innes was talking.

"It was a perfectly logical decision," he said to Beth, over Snib's head.

"It was unbelievably dangerous!" Beth yelled back.

"Stop arguing," said Molly. "We have to see if Snib's ok. Is your arm hurt?"

Snib nodded and winced. "Are you alright, Molly?"

"Bashed and bruised, but everything's still working. Are you fine apart from your arm? Is your head ok?"

"Yes. And Innes hasn't stopped arguing since I sat up, so I think he's fine too."

Innes shrugged. "We have to get the star iron. There's no time to waste."

"The star iron is gone," said Molly. "But Snib is right here and she's injured. We have to help her first."

Innes sighed and looked at Beth. "You heal trees, can you have a look?"

Beth muttered, "I suppose so," then knelt beside Snib and pulled the crow-girl's cardigan sleeve off, to show an arm already purpled with bruising.

"It's not bent," said Molly. "Is that a good sign?"

Beth nodded. "It's not broken, but I'll need a splint so I can use the energy of the wood to help her heal. Someone find me a branch, please. Fallen wood only, from a naturally healthy tree, not these tortured ones."

"I'll go," said Molly.

"I'll come with you," said Innes. "I want to see if any bits of me fall off when I move."

They walked out of the castle courtyard, towards the nearest patch of leafless winter trees.

"Are you really ok?" asked Molly.

"More embarrassed than sore," replied Innes. "I was the first to fall. You fell further than me, because you climbed highest. Are you sure you're fine?"

Molly rolled her shoulders. "I'll have a few bruises tomorrow morning, that's all."

They reached the trees and Molly scuffed her feet through the undergrowth. She picked up a long straight stick. Innes took it and snapped it between his hands.

"Hey!"

"If it's that easy to snap, it won't be any use. Not flexible. No life left."

They found crooked sticks, short sticks and thorny sticks. Then Molly found a smooth branch, just longer than Snib's forearm.

Innes flexed it gently. "That's fresh enough."

They walked back to the ruins and Beth smiled at the stick. "Perfect, thanks."

"How do we tie it onto her arm?" asked Molly. "Does anyone have bandages or a sling?"

Innes laughed. "Don't be daft. No one carries that sort of thing around."

Molly said, "Should we rip up someone's t-shirt?"

"You're not wrecking any of my clothes," said Innes. "You can have my socks."

"I don't want your smelly socks on my arm!" said Snib, with a tinge of pink in her cheeks at last.

"He's right," said Molly. "We don't have anything else." She pulled off her boots, then her long warm socks. She put the cold hard boots back on her bare feet.

Beth laid the branch along the outside of Snib's arm. The dryad ran her hand carefully along the branch towards Snib's elbow, then ran it back again along Snib's skin. Snib gasped, then sighed.

Molly held the branch steady while Beth tied Molly's stripy socks round Snib's elbow and wrist, and one of Innes's socks in the middle of her forearm.

"Thank you," said Snib. "It feels better already."

Molly buttoned Snib's cardi to hold her arm close to her chest.

Theo said, "Now let's get the star iron."

"But the star iron has gone," said Molly.

"No it hasn't," said Beth. "These two *idiots* have something to tell you." She waved her hand at Innes and Theo.

Theo looked embarrassed. "That shiny rock wasn't the star iron. I sort of pointed at the wrong rock in the cabinet, as a bit of misdirection."

Molly rubbed her bruised shoulder. "Did we all just climb up and fall down a ruined castle for a rock we didn't need?"

"Yes. Sorry. The fungus fairies were actually holding a lump of fool's gold."

Molly sighed. "Did you know we were chasing fool's gold, Innes? You'd seen the star iron before."

"Yes." He shrugged. "I tried to correct toad-boy in the tower, but he kicked me. Quite hard. Then I worked out what he was doing, so I shut up."

"Who else knew? While I was climbing past slimy sneezing fungi, who else knew?"

"I knew by then," said Atacama, "and we had to tell Beth eventually."

"That's why we were *all* shouting at you to come down," said Beth. "But you didn't pay any attention."

"I didn't pay any attention, because I thought I was trying to get the object that could save all those curse victims from the Promise Keeper. But if the fairies had the wrong rock, why did *any* of us climb up?"

"By risking ourselves for it," said Theo, "we convinced the fungus fairies they had the right stone. Now they've escaped with the fool's gold, we can get the real star iron. I kept saying 'We have to *try*', but you didn't realise what I meant. Sorry."

"And why..." asked Snib in a small voice at their feet, "why did you lie about it at all? Why did you think 'misdirection' was necessary? Who were you trying to fool with that fool's gold? When I had Molly-mouse in my pocket, saving her from that clawy cat, did you think I was about to run to Corbie and tell him everything?"

161

Innes said, "*Someone* told Corbie we were on a quest for that glittery rock. That's why the fungus fairies had the wrong one."

Snib held her arm and sniffed. "You think it was me?"

Molly crouched beside her. "I don't think it was you." She looked up at her friends. "It could have been the fungus fairies. They could have been hiding in the tower. We talked about the star iron outside too. Any bird flying overhead, any creature hiding in the shadows, could have heard us. There's no reason to think it was Snib, and every reason to think it wasn't. Look at her! She risked herself as much as any of us, and injured herself more, trying to get that rock from the fungus fairies."

Molly helped Snib to her feet. "We need to get the star iron, before someone recognises the rock as fool's gold. And this time, we're all going to trust each other, aren't we?"

No one spoke, no one moved. No one agreed with her.

"Oh come on! We've all seen how miserable Snib is about the crows' link to curses, how scared she is for her brothers and sisters. So I choose to trust her."

Atacama nodded. "Lots of other creatures could have spied on us. I'll trust the crow-girl."

Innes said, "She was as brave as the rest of us climbing that wall. I'll trust her."

Beth shrugged. "I'm not sure if I trust her, but she can't do us much harm with that injured arm, and whether I trust her or not, Molly's right, we have to get that star iron now."

"Fine," said Theo. "When I pointed to the wrong rock, I was just being cautious."

"We can't climb the slime wall again," said Molly, "so I'm going in the front door."

Everyone followed Molly round to the carved door.

Innes grinned. "Great. I'll kick it in."

"No, you won't. I'm going through that hole there." Molly pointed to a tiny gap at the base of the door, where two planks curved away from each other. "I'll get in as a mouse, then shift back and walk up the stairs."

She held her hand out. "Cabinet key please."

Innes stared at her for a moment, then handed her the key. Molly zipped it into her coat pocket, knowing that anything she put in her pockets before becoming an animal would still be there when she shifted back to human.

"And what does the star iron *actually* look like? Now we're all being honest with each other."

Theo said, "It's grey, knobbly and slightly burnt."

Innes added, "It's the most boring-looking rock in there. It's on the bottom shelf, between a fossilised fern and a tarnished medal. But are you sure you should go in, Molly? What about the cat?"

"If he makes a noise, I'll become a mouse, make a boundary and jump over it. It's fine. We don't want any watching crows to know we're breaking in. And a mouse is quick and quiet. Who's going to miaow for me?"

"Don't anyone dare miaow!" said Beth. "This is ridiculous. It's far too dangerous."

Molly said, "A curse army is slightly more dangerous than a Siamese cat. This is the simplest way to get one of the few objects on the planet that can stop Estelle and whatever monsters and victims she's creating with her charged-up curses. I'm going in. Atacama?"

The sphinx purred.

Molly became a mouse.

Instantly nervous of the wide sky and huge landscape, she darted between paws and boots and trainers, and dashed through the mouse-sized hole at the bottom of the gigantic door.

She was back in Ballindreich House. On her own.

Molly couldn't draw a boundary line on the stone floor of the corridor, so she darted along beside the skirting board, into the first room with a wooden floor. She used her sharp claws to score a line in the varnish, imagining the speed and power of her hare's back legs. Then she looked at this wood and that wood, and lifted her paw up.

She jumped.

And she rolled, just missing the metal stand supporting the golden rope.

She was a girl again. With a key in her pocket. After breaking the line with her thumbnail, she moved fast through the house, past the family portraits and leather-bound books, then ran up the stairs.

She reached the tower room, ducked under the rope and walked to the cabinet of curiosities. It was like an old bookcase, with four shelves behind a glass door. But it didn't contain books. It contained an odd mix of objects; each one sitting beside a faded label.

There was a jagged hole in the glass. The fungus fairies weren't tidy burglars.

On the top shelf, she saw a sword hilt with a broken blade, a yellowy scrap of lace labelled:

> From the last dress worn
> by Mary Queen of Scots

and a gap in the light dust beside a label that said:

> Fool's gold, or iron pyrite

Perhaps fungus fairies couldn't read.

On the next shelf, her eye was caught by a long toothy jawbone labelled:

> From the last wolf
> in Scotland

On the second bottom shelf, she noticed a delicate bracelet of cowrie shells, and a long thick leather collar, studded with iron nails, labelled:

> A faery dog collar, can
> control hounds of the Sidh

On the bottom shelf, there was a slate marked with a ghostly fern, a medal on a stripy ribbon, and a fist-sized lump of dull grey rock. It wasn't labelled 'star iron'. The label read:

A meteorite from inside the Arctic Circle, discovered by Lord Fergus Algernon Hamilton Duff

Molly unlocked the door and opened it, stepping back when a slice of broken glass fell out and crashed to the floor.

She lifted out the meteorite. "It's not stealing," she whispered to herself. "We'll send it back to the people who really found it." She put the star iron in the left pocket of her coat and zipped it up.

Her eye was drawn to the beautiful little cowrie bracelet. She stroked it, thinking Rosalind would love it. But she couldn't take a stolen present to a birthday party.

She looked again at the object beside it. The faery dog collar. The collar that could control a hound of the Sidh.

Molly wasn't sure she believed that the lace was from Mary Queen of Scots' dress, or that the jawbone was from the last wolf, and she knew that Lord Fergus Algernon Hamilton Duff hadn't discovered the star iron on his own. Could she believe that this collar would control a faery dog, a deephound? That it would give her power over Mr Crottel?

She touched it. The leather was cold, greasy and almost scaly, with raised diamond-shapes along its length. It was much longer than an ordinary dog collar, coiled up like a snake or a whip. The nails were driven right through the collar: wide heads on the outside, sharp points jutting through the inside. The buckle was plain and square. A vicious collar, for a vicious dog.

Molly couldn't steal for a birthday present. Could she steal to save her own life? Was her safety more important than tourists glancing at a collar they probably didn't believe in anyway?

She picked up the coiled collar, put it in her right pocket, and zipped the pocket closed, feeling an instant sweat of guilt down her back.

As she locked the broken door and slid the key into her jeans pocket, she looked at the gap on the shelf. Should she put the collar back? Was it right to commit a crime to escape a curse?

Then, behind her, she heard the cat miaow.

Chapter Eighteen

Molly flung herself under the cabinet as she shifted, and cowered there in her shivering mouse form.

She saw the cat, stepping slowly and elegantly towards her.

Molly wanted to run and hide. The base of the cabinet wasn't low enough to keep her safe. She wanted to squeeze into a hole in the wall or a gap in the floorboards – into any space too small for a cat's paw.

But if Molly hid in a mousehole, she would be trapped as a mouse. She needed to find a space big enough to shift in, with enough time to draw and jump a boundary.

However, there was a cat between Molly and clear space. And that cat was stretching his claws under the cabinet to drag Molly out.

Molly decided to fight the fear shaking her body. The fear that every mouse feels when faced by a cat. The fear that forces every mouse to run away. The fear that every cat relies on.

Molly decided not to be afraid. She wasn't a mouse.

She didn't have to think like a mouse or act like a mouse.

So Molly bit the cat's approaching paw. One swift nip with her tiny teeth.

The cat jerked his paw away.

Molly ran out of cover, right at the cat.

The cat backed off.

Molly ran straight towards the cat, leapt at him, scrabbled up over his surprised cream-and-brown face, jumped between his ears and scampered along his spine. She jumped off the cat's skinny tail, and ran right out the door.

Molly leapt down the stairs. Her mouse body was light and nimble, her judgement of speed and distance had been honed by months of racing as a hare. So she bounced fast and accurately off each step.

Behind her, she could hear soft paws on the stone steps. The cat was racing after her.

But Molly didn't lose races. Not to anyone. Not even as a mouse.

She altered her line, to take her to the outer edge of the curved staircase. She slowed down, to let the cat catch up.

She tempted the cat to pounce at her.

As soon as the cat pounced, Molly turned as sharply as a dodging hare, and ducked into the nearest doorway. The cat missed his footing and tumbled down the next couple of steps.

Molly ran into the nursery. She saw a stripy red-and-yellow rug. She pulled her paw along the nearest red woolly stripe, remembering her straight run at the cat and imagining the wool on either side coming from different sheep, then she lifted her paw and leapt the line.

She landed on the rug as a girl, her first soft landing for days. She somersaulted and leapt to her feet.

And saw a surprised Siamese cat in the doorway.

Molly bent down and looked the cat in the eye. The cat stared at her. Molly stared back. The cat blinked.

Molly smiled. "Yes. I'm a girl, not a mouse. And I can do magic. So I think you should run away *now*!" She clapped her hands, and the cat ran to hide under a cot in the corner of the nursery.

Molly walked briskly down the stairs, with the star iron in one pocket and the faery dog collar in the other.

As her heels drummed along the corridor, she realised that if this collar could control Mr Crottel, then she could finally force him to lift her curse. If this really was a magical collar, she wouldn't have to keep asking politely, knowing he would refuse every time. She might now have the power to be free of her curse.

But did she want to be free of it?

She frowned as she hung the cabinet key back on the rack. Did she want to lose her curse, or keep it?

She didn't have to decide yet. First she had to get this star iron to the Promise Keeper, to force her to take the extra power out of charged-up curses.

Molly strode to the front door. It was locked.

She laughed, then miaowed loudly, wondering if that would work. And it did.

Because Molly was now completely in control of her curse.

She could become a hare whenever she chose. She could shift back to a girl by creating a boundary. She could even, if she wanted, shift to and from other animals. She now controlled her curse, rather her curse controlling her.

So she would probably never need this collar.

Molly left the house the same way she'd entered – as a tiny mouse – then created a quick boundary on the ground and leapt over it.

She stood up, in the middle of her friends, with a big grin.

"You didn't meet the cat then," said Atacama.

"Oh yes. I met him, and I taught him to be more careful which mice he chases. And I got the star iron." She unzipped the left pocket and handed the meteorite to Theo.

Molly thought about showing them the collar as well, but decided that it was her choice whether to use it or not, so she would keep it her secret for now.

Theo lifted the meteorite up and down, weighing it in his hand. He nodded. "I can feel something very slightly different..." He rolled the stone around in both hands. "A different vibration, perhaps. This definitely contains something not normally found on Earth. An element that will disrupt the Promise Keeper's balance, force her to withdraw her excess power from the curses to protect herself."

He smiled at Molly. "And you realise a hare couldn't have got through that gap in the door? By charging up your curse, Estelle gave you the ability to collect the object that can stop her charging up everyone's curses. I love it when magic moves in circles!"

They all turned towards the bike shelter.

The empty bike shelter.

"Where's my bike? Where's my aunt's bike?" Molly looked round at everyone. "Did someone steal them while you were all standing here? Didn't you notice?"

Beth said, "Sorry. We were concentrating on the house. Innes was ready to kick the door in if we heard anything worrying."

Molly shook her head. "A cat catching a mouse at the top of a tower would have been a very quiet end to our quest. You wouldn't have heard anything." She sighed. "Now we've lost the bikes. Do you think the curse-hatched took them?"

"It doesn't matter who took them," said Atacama. "Presumably someone who doesn't want us to weaken the Promise Keeper. Whoever it was, the bikes have gone, so we have to get back to Craigvenie without them."

Innes said, "I can't carry four of you at once. I could manage two, then come back for the others. Atacama can manage himself, of course."

Theo said, "I don't think we should split up. We should stay together, keep each other safe."

"Keep an eye on each other," muttered Beth, glancing at Snib.

Molly said, "It'll take a while to walk back to Craigvenie. How far is it? About ten miles?"

"It's not nearly that far, as the crow flies," said Snib, with a small smile. "Over the moors, rather than by road, it's half that distance."

Beth looked at the sky. "Those clouds are heavy." She blew a fast breath out and they all saw it whiten in the air. "And it's cold enough that if the clouds open, it might fall as snow or hail."

Innes looked round. "Everyone has coats or cloaks or fur. We'll be fine."

As they left the Ballindreich grounds and headed towards the hills, Molly asked, "How exactly do we weaken the Promise Keeper with the star iron?"

Theo said, "We have to make sure that Estelle touches it."

"We'll have to trick her," said Innes. "We could offer to watch that nasty Curse TV with her, and hide the star iron in a bowl of popcorn, then she might dig her hand right down and brush against it."

"Or we could play a game of catch, and throw it to her," said Atacama.

"She doesn't play games any more," said Molly.

"We don't have to trick her," said Theo. "We could simply give it to her, as a present. As tribute. We could tie a ribbon round it."

Snib said, "We could wrap it in shiny paper, so she unwraps it and is holding it before she works out what it is."

They all agreed that Snib's idea was the best so far, and Theo slipped the rock inside his tunic.

As they trudged across the winter heather on the hills

between Ballindreich and Craigvenie, Molly noticed that the puddles of water on the path were freezing over. They walked faster to keep warm.

Then it started to snow.

Molly loved snow. In Edinburgh, snow was rare and exciting. Even a light snowfall was worth running around in, catching flakes on her tongue. Thick snow meant snowball fights, snowmen and maybe even a day off school. She loved snow on the hills too, looking at the white caps and blue shadows from the car.

But snow falling on her shoulders when she was miles from shelter seemed threatening and dangerous rather than fun.

Beth said, "Stay close together. Keep an eye on each other. And this time I don't mean 'watch Snib'. I mean take care of each other. Let's not lose anyone."

As they walked, snowflakes filled the air, settling like tiny diamonds on Theo's glossy black hair and Atacama's thick black fur, and covering the ground in icing-sugar swirls.

Molly saw a perfect six-pronged flake land on her cuff. Suddenly tempted, she lifted her head and stuck her tongue out to catch one of the flakes spiralling in front of her.

She flinched.

The flake had stung her. It was cold, of course, but it was also sharp.

She held her hand up to catch another flake. A delicate white shape tumbled onto her palm and stuck there.

She blew at it, but it didn't move. It stayed, one edge caught in her skin. As the flake melted, a red bead of blood rose from the palm of her hand.

She looked at Innes. He had a line of blood on his cheekbone.

Molly called out, "The snow is attacking us!"

The snow fell faster, whirled and thrown by gusts of wind. They all huddled together, overlapping coats and cloaks and cardigans to build a tent over their heads.

Beth gasped, "These snowflakes are like tiny knives."

"Six-bladed knives!" said Innes. "But we can't just cower here."

"Cowering seems safer than going out in that," said Snib.

"It's not freak weather," said Innes. "We're being ambushed. We have to fight back or escape."

Theo said, "It's not strong magic. The ice is sharp, but localised. Let's cover up as much skin as we can and push through it."

"I'll lead the way," said Atacama. "It's not getting through my fur, so I only have to guard my eyes. Follow me, fast."

After a quick kerfuffle of hoods and hats to make sure everyone's faces were covered, they broke apart and started to run.

They ran right into a wall of whirling snow-blades, which sliced at their flimsy fabric shields as the wind battered at them.

They pushed through, the sphinx cutting through

the snow ahead, followed by everyone else. Molly felt the wind punch her belly and shoulders, but she kept following.

The snow began to fall even faster and heavier, pummelling and pushing them all towards the ground.

Molly tried to keep running, but her feet slipped and she fell, landing hard on Snib, who was already curled up and sobbing.

Molly tried to stand, but the snow lay on top of her like freezing paving stones. She was trapped on the ground.

The snow slowed. Now, instead of tiny white shapes spiralling from the sky, huge black shapes dived down towards them.

Huge black birds.

Chapter Nineteen

The black birds swooped down on Molly and her friends, grasped them with sharp talons and lifted them high into the air.

But these birds weren't crows. These birds were long-necked, bald-headed, hook-beaked vultures. Giant vultures, big enough to lift a sphinx and a newly shifted horse.

Definitely big enough to lift Molly, Beth and Theo.

But Snib was left on the ground, a sobbing ball of wet rags.

The vultures holding the five friends flew slowly in a circle centred on a tall man standing below.

Corbie. The leader of the curse-hatched.

Outside the circle of vultures flew a wider ring of black birds: crows, buzzards and eagles.

High above flew an even bigger black bird, which had scaly legs as thick as pine trees and single feathers as wide as school desks. Molly was reminded of Sinbad stories about birds big enough to carry away elephants.

The bird screeched.

Molly hoped briefly that the screech would turn her into an elephant so she could land hard on Corbie.

Corbie laughed at her. "Do you like my roc? She's our biggest curse-hatched yet! But she won't turn you into anything useful, if that's what you're hoping. You won't shift at all when you hear a roc call, because rocs hunt human beings. You're already her prey!"

Corbie looked round at everyone dangling from the vultures' talons. "Who has the star iron? Who has the stone I can use to threaten that frivolous Promise Keeper, so she will charge up the right curses to build my curse army?"

He waved his hand towards a ring of people and creatures. As Molly was dragged through the cold air, she glimpsed a woman in a cloak of snowflakes, a handful of earthbound human curse-hatched, a horned wyrm and three pale blobs that could be fungus fairies. She also saw a huge green dog and a scarred grey horse.

Corbie grinned. "You see the first recruits to the army my mother imagined, the army that will give power to the curse-hatched and make revenge the most potent magic in the world. But first I need the star iron. So, who has it?"

No one said anything. No one pointed at Theo, no one even glanced at him. They all looked at the massive roc above them, or the shabby curse-hatched leader below.

Corbie crouched down, brushed the snow from Snib's shivering shoulders, and said, "Tell me, sister. Who has it?"

Snib sat up, Snib smiled, and Snib pointed at Theo.

The crow-girl said, "The magician has it, Corbie. And,

like I told you, he can't use magic to defend it, so you can just take it from him."

Corbie looked up at Theo. "You are a magician with power you're afraid to use. I am the commander of a curse army that I'm quite happy to use. This is not a contest of equals. You will give me what I want."

"It's not a very big curse army," said Theo calmly. "More of a curse gang. I'm not impressed. And I'm not giving you anything."

Corbie nodded to the wide ring of black birds.

Suddenly Theo was mobbed by dozens of crows, buzzards and eagles, all flapping and pecking and clawing at him. Shreds of his cloak floated out of the whirlwind of feathers.

Molly saw Theo's face harden and saw him raise his hands as high as he could while his shoulders were held by a giant vulture.

She knew that Theo could stop the birds' attack with a few gestures of those powerful hands. She'd seen him create weapons from the air and throw monsters into the sea. But she also knew that if he used his power, he wouldn't just destroy his attackers. He would destroy everyone and everything around him. He would destroy his friends as well as his enemies.

Molly held her breath.

Through the blur of feathers and beaks, she saw Theo close his eyes and let his hands drop. Then he wrapped his cloak around himself and over the star iron in his tunic.

But the birds jabbed and tugged and pecked and scratched. They ripped his cloak, dragged his arms apart and shredded his tunic.

The dull grey lump of star iron tumbled out and dropped towards the ground. It landed deep in a drift of snow, digging its own dark hole as it fell.

The mobbing birds flapped away from Theo and he hung, motionless, from the vulture's talons.

Corbie lifted the star iron from the snow. "The fool's gold was prettier, but this is the rock with power. Thanks magician, for realising what it could do; thanks hare-girl, for fetching it. Now I will control the Promise Keeper and the curse arc. I will have even more power than my mother did."

Molly looked down at Snib, who was clambering to her feet. "Snib! Were you spying on us all the time?"

Snib looked straight at Molly. No tears, no sniffling, no cowering or cringing. "Of course I was. Don't sound so surprised, Molly. I told you what I was doing, right from the start."

"You said you were sent to spy on us, but you also said you didn't want to!"

"I didn't want to. That was true. I didn't want to spend time with you. But I did what I was told. I spied on you. I wrote down all your conversations and plans, then I left little notes for my sisters and brothers to pick up. I left messages on roofs, on walls, on the ground. You never noticed, because you wanted to trust me. You're weak and foolish in many ways, Molly-mouse, but your greatest weakness is your need to trust your friends."

Molly said, "That's not a weakness. My mistake was believing you were my friend."

"How could I *ever* be your friend? You killed my mother."

Molly stared at Snib, and realised it was true. She'd thought of Snib as Corbie's little sister and Mickle's big sister, but never as Nan's daughter.

"I'm sorry."

"Are you?" asked Snib.

Innes shifted back to a boy to shout, "Traitor!"

"At least I'm not a traitor to my family, like you."

Beth yelled, "I never trusted you."

Snib smiled. "But you went along with everyone else. You even fixed my arm for me." She pulled off the socks, let the splint fall to the ground and flexed her arm. "Thanks for that."

Theo said hoarsely, "But your brothers and sisters are still under threat, as their curses become more dangerous."

Snib shrugged. "We all have to make sacrifices."

Corbie said, "We're done here. Drop them."

The vultures opened their talons. Not one of Molly's friends fell in a soft snowdrift. All of them fell onto icy heather or hard stones.

Snib stood over Molly. "I can still fly, you know. You never truly defeated us, because I can still fly." She stretched out her arms. Two eagles flew down and grasped her wrists.

The eagles lifted Snib into the air, and began to fly away.

Molly yelled after her, "That's not really flying, Snib. You know it isn't!"

The circling birds screeched. The new recruits growled and snarled and hissed. They all moved towards Molly and her friends.

But Corbie said, "No, just leave them lying on the cold ground, with only their misery and shame to keep them warm. They aren't worth our time or energy." He kicked Theo, and laughed. "You are all completely pathetic. You can't tell a friend from an enemy, you can't hold onto a magical object for more than a few minutes, and your strongest team member is a useless embarrassment. So now I will have my revenge: you must watch my curse army darken your world, using the power *you* brought us!"

Corbie was lifted up by the roc, whose massive wings blew a blizzard of sharp flakes round the group huddled on the ground.

As the army flapped and marched and slithered away, Molly heard again, "I can still fly," and Snib vanished into the clouds.

Chapter Twenty

Molly's curse was completely confused by the chorus of birdcalls, hisses and snarls as the army left. By the time she was watching Snib fade into the clouds, Molly was perched on top of the snowy heather as…

Actually, Molly had no idea what she was, but she was aware of lots of legs and a hunger for spinach.

She heard Beth's booming voice. "For earth's sake. Now she's a caterpillar."

A huge white shape gouged a trench in front of her, then large wet fangs picked her up and carried her over the line.

Molly was human again.

She looked at Innes, who'd drawn a line with his hoof, and Atacama, who'd lifted her over it, said "Thanks," and smiled.

No one else was smiling.

Everyone was dotted with cuts from the snow-blades. Everyone had rips in their coats or lumps of fur missing, after being grasped by the vultures' talons. Everyone was bruised from their falls to the ground.

But Theo had suffered the most. His cloak and tunic were bloodstained and shredded. His hands and chest were grazed from the beaks of the mobbing birds. He was crouched on the ground, his face raised to the sky, as he began to scream.

One long raw scream of a vowel. No words. Just anger and frustration...

Theo raised his hands to thump them on the ground. Then he jerked the motion backwards and hit himself instead, punching his legs, as if he was afraid to touch the earth with his hands, in case he accidentally used his magic.

He yelled again and again.

Molly, Innes, Beth and Atacama stood together and watched him.

"How can we help him?" asked Molly.

"I don't think we can," said Innes. "Not yet. We just have to let him get it out."

Theo screamed so long and so loud that the clouds above him parted, letting a shaft of sunlight through.

He stared at the hole in the grey sky, and whispered, "I have to be so careful... all the time."

He put his head in his hands.

Innes walked over and touched Theo's shoulder. "I'm sorry."

"No, I'm the one who's sorry. Corbie's right. I am useless. I can do nothing. Nothing to protect my friends. Nothing to protect the curse arc. Nothing to protect the *world*."

Theo looked up and there were tears in his dark eyes. "I can't do anything without making everything worse. And I nearly gave in. I nearly attacked Corbie. I nearly defended myself. That would have been so selfish. It would have destroyed you all. I would have been left standing, alone, on a pile of rubble. But I nearly did it because I was angry. Because I was threatened." He looked down again and muttered, "Because I was scared."

Innes said, "But you didn't. You're not like Estelle, you don't use your power just because you can. And you're not useless. Your knowledge and your courage are just as important to us as your strength and your magic. You're not useless."

They all sat down beside Theo, huddling together for warmth and comfort.

Atacama sighed. "I saw the deephound in Corbie's little band of nasties. So we know where Molly's curse-caster is."

Molly touched her right pocket, and nodded.

"I saw the fungus fairies," said Beth.

"And the weather witch who made the snow-blades," said Theo.

"Anyone else?" asked Innes quietly. "Did any of you recognise anyone else?"

There was silence.

"Or was it just me who saw the horse?"

Molly pulled her socks back on. "Yes, I saw your dad. So we know where he is too."

Innes shivered. "Now all our enemies are working together. And we just gave them more power."

"I'm so sorry!" moaned Theo.

"It wasn't your fault," said Innes. "It was all of us. Crossing the moor in this weather was stupid. Letting a curse-hatched know our plans was even more stupid. We're complete idiots."

"Snib was my fault," said Molly. "I wanted to trust her. I wanted you all to trust her. She seemed so sad, and she talked about flying the way I feel about running. I think that convinced me to trust her. Sorry."

"Don't blame yourself," said Atacama. "We were all taken in, especially after she'd injured herself falling from the wall."

Molly shook her head. "I even knew she had a pencil and paper in her pocket. I wanted to gnaw the pencil when I was a mouse. I can't believe I didn't realise what it was for. I'm sorry."

"Ok," said Beth, standing up and brushing snow from her legs. "We're all sorry, and we're all idiots. But we're not achieving anything sitting here. Let's get up, get to Craigvenie and work out what to do next."

As they walked, Molly felt the heavy leather collar in her pocket banging against her bruised hip. She started to ask, "Atacama, what do you know about..." then she realised everyone was looking at her, hopeful she had an idea.

If she asked about the collar, she'd have to use the collar.

Or, at least, she'd have to listen to Beth nagging her to use the collar. She hesitated.

"What do I know about what?" asked the sphinx.

"Em… a box! Do you know anything about a box?"

"What kind of box?"

"Mrs Sharpe mentioned a box," said Molly. "She told me to ask the crow about the box. She said that was the way to stop the Keeper."

"Did you ask the crow?" said Beth.

"Yes, but she claimed she didn't know anything about any boxes. So, with all your ancient learning and your family lore, do any of you know of a box that could help us stop Estelle now, before Corbie gets to her?"

Beth frowned. "Why didn't you mention this box before?"

Molly shrugged. "The star iron seemed like the best plan. I didn't want to send us on two different quests at the same time. But the box idea is all I have now." She prodded her pocket. It wasn't all she had. But the collar would only save her, not anyone else.

"So, what do we know?" said Theo, sounding more like himself now he had a magical problem to consider. "It's a box, which Mrs Sharpe has reason to believe contains something that can help us stop Estelle."

"And which a crow – perhaps any of the crows, or just that one treacherous crow – knows about," said Innes.

"We can't ask Snib," said Beth, "because we won't be talking to *her* ever again."

"So where might the box be?" asked Theo.

"The Keeper's Hall?" suggested Molly.

Innes shook his head. "If there was something at the Hall that Mrs Sharpe could use to stop Estelle bullying her, I'm sure she'd have used it by now."

"Could it be in Stone Egg Wood?" wondered Beth, as they slid down a steep slope. "Maybe that's why she mentioned the crow."

"If there's a box at Stone Egg Wood, it won't be easy to get," said Theo. "That's where Corbie has barracked his nasty little army."

"Where else could it be?" asked Atacama.

Innes said, "There are boxes everywhere: shops, warehouses, attics…"

Beth said, "We can look for the box in the morning, when it's light and when we aren't too tired and bruised to think. First we all need to warm up, eat something and get some sleep. My house is nearest, so—"

Atacama hissed, "Shhh! Down!"

They all dropped into the heather.

The sphinx pointed at the brow of the next hill. They crawled up and peered over.

They saw a line of fabled beasts walking below them, heading southwest.

Molly saw two familiar boys, arms linked, faces pale and tired, beetles and gems falling from their lips.

Behind them walked a troll with a rusty axe, a giant goat with dozens of horns, a centaur filly with glass hooves slicing into the path, a pure white minotaur, a weeping girl wearing a dress made of thistles, and a wolf with a boy's head who kept flickering into a boy with a wolf's head.

Molly heard a high-pitched sob from behind her. She turned round and saw a fairy in a woolly yellow dress, fluttering in the wind.

Molly slid back down the slope a little, so she wasn't visible to the fabled beasts on the other side of the hill, then sat up. Her friends followed her.

The fairy said, "Don't mind me, I'm just... I'm just on my way to sanctuary..."

"You're shaking with tiredness." Beth held out her hand. "Rest for a minute."

"No. I can't land, so I can't rest."

"Why not?"

"Because..." the fairy sobbed again, "because I've been cursed!"

"We've all been cursed," said Molly. "Tell us about yours."

"I'm a daffodil fairy. A couple of years ago, I offended a primrose fairy by saying that my yellow was the true yellow of spring, and she cursed me so that whenever I land on one of my own flowers it withers and dies. That was horrible enough, but recently everything I land on – snowdrops, trees, grass, *every* plant I land on – dies. I don't even want to know what would happen if I landed on animals, or people, or dryads... So I can't land. I can't ever land."

"Yes, you can." Theo scrabbled under the heather and

pulled out a rock. He brushed the earth off and laid it flat on the ground. "You can't kill stone. Land on this."

The fairy fell out of the air so fast she almost rolled off the rock. But she righted herself and perched on the top, then sighed in relief.

"Can't you ask the primrose fairy to lift the curse?" suggested Molly. "She won't want you to kill everything you land on: it puts her own flowers at risk too."

"I'm sure she would lift it, but she won't be easy to find until her flowers start to bloom, which could be weeks away."

"Are they all seeking sanctuary too?" Innes pointed over his shoulder. "The beetle-spitting boys, the wolf boy, the jaggy girl and all those monsters?"

The fairy nodded. "We've been summoned: victims whose curses have become enhanced, and casters who enjoy seeing their curses get stronger and don't want to be forced to lift them. We've been summoned and offered sanctuary. We'll be safe from those who're horrified by our curses, and all we have to do in return is fight for Corbie. I'll be able to rest, because I can't kill the fossilised trees in Stone Egg Wood."

"But you don't want to be part of a curse army, do you?" asked Molly.

"I'm sure no one will actually expect me to fight," said the fairy. "What use would I be? I'm only going because the other fairies shout at me when I hover near their plants."

Atacama said, "But if you kill every plant you land on,

then you could be a dangerous weapon. Corbie will use that. He will use you."

The fairy frowned, then fluttered up into the air. "Thanks for the rock and the rest, but I have to go. We've been asked to prepare for the welcome feast tomorrow, and I don't want to be late."

"Please don't go," said Beth. "Don't let him turn your curse into a weapon. Flower fairies aren't soldiers."

"I've killed too many flowers to deserve the name 'flower fairy' any more. I must go to Stone Egg Wood and learn how to live with my curse."

She flew away.

Innes said, "Corbie is building his bigger army."

"We have to find that box," said Molly. "And hope whatever's inside is more powerful than all those creatures marching towards Stone Egg Wood."

Chapter Twenty-One

As the cold afternoon faded into an icy evening, Molly and her friends trudged over the moors, then down the lower slopes into the fields, across a shallow river and towards Beth's woods.

"Are you sure you want to take us into your woods?" asked Molly. "You said you didn't want me to endanger your trees again."

Beth sighed. "I was too upset by my injured tree to think clearly yesterday. I know you're doing the right thing, trying to stop the Keeper and Corbie. I want to do the right thing too."

So Beth led them all to her wooden house. "We were ambushed by crows again," she told her Aunt Jean as they walked into the kitchen. "Everyone needs to eat, and Theo needs to borrow more sensible clothes."

Jean looked up from the bowl she was stirring. "You're all welcome to stay the night. I'll call Doreen and tell her you're here, if you want, Molly?"

Molly nodded. "Thanks."

Innes said, "Do I smell cake?"

"That's not cake for *now*, that's cake for later." Rosalind bounced out from under the table. "We're baking for my birthday party tomorrow! The first cake got a bit burnt, and the second cake got a bit dropped on the floor. But this cake will be just right!"

Beth said, "I'm sure it will be lovely." She picked Rosalind up and birled her round, then said, "Aunt Jean, do you know anything about a mysterious box, possibly connected to Mrs Sharpe or the crows of Stone Egg Wood or the Promise Keeper?"

Her aunt frowned. "I don't think so."

Beth led her friends upstairs, with Rosalind chasing after them.

"Have you got me a present yet? What have you got me? You're not meant to tell me, so don't tell me, but give me a clue. Have you got anything yet?"

Innes said, "Yes, we've got something. But it's locked in a cage, so it doesn't eat anyone before your party."

Rosalind shrieked, then giggled and ran back downstairs.

"We still don't have a real present for her," said Molly.

Beth said, "That's hardly our main problem. We don't know where to look for that mysterious box tomorrow."

Beth had a big room, so there was plenty of space for the duvets, cushions, pillows and quilts that she heaped up, and for the tray of hot chocolate and slightly burnt cake that Jean brought for supper.

"I'm too tired to eat," said Innes. "I just want to sleep."

Then he ate half the cake before lying down.

Atacama curled up and started to snore. Molly tensed and waited for the flash of heat. But it didn't come. Apparently snoring wasn't a predatory enough noise to turn her into a goat.

As she lay there, snug under a patchwork quilt, she listened to Atacama's snores and to Innes and Theo whispering sleepily on the other side of the room. She thought about Snib, who'd been lying on her own floor last night.

Molly had trusted Snib. She'd liked her.

But she wondered if she could believe anything the crow-girl had said.

Snib had said that Mr Crottel was at Stone Egg Wood. That was true, because Molly had seen the deephound with Corbie's recruits.

Snib had said that the name of Molly's curse-hatched was Mickle. That might be true, too.

Snib had said that she wished someone would break the link between curse-hatched and curses. Her voice had sounded so sad, so hopeful, Molly couldn't believe that wasn't true.

But if any of what Snib had said was true – if she wanted to save her brothers and sisters from Corbie's ambition, if she didn't want to be linked to curses, if she cared about curse victims – then why had she spied for Corbie? Why had she made friends with Molly, then betrayed her? Why had she betrayed the whole team?

Molly sighed. She sat up in her warm quilt nest and leant on the edge of Beth's pine bed. Beth was awake, looking out of her window at the stars framed by the branches around the house.

Molly whispered, "I'm sorry. I'm sorry the smelly green dog bit your tree, I'm sorry I trusted Snib and I'm sorry I never quite manage to get rid of my curse."

Beth said, "I'm sorry too. I'm sorry I nag you about your curse. I do know it's not the darkness you like, it's the speed."

She smiled at Molly, then yawned.

Molly grinned back. "Night night, then."

Beth said, "Sleep tight. If you can, with Atacama snoring…"

But they slept soundly all night.

And Rosalind woke them in the morning. "Wakey wakey! Time to go on a quest for my birthday present!"

They sat up and sang her a slightly out-of-tune 'Happy Birthday to You'.

Atacama stretched, wiped his paws over his face and ears, and said, "Well, I'm ready." The rest of them took turns having a quick wash in the bathroom, and Beth borrowed clothes from her uncles to replace Theo's ripped tunic and cloak. He didn't look quite so exotic in a blue jumper and grey fleece.

"Breakfast, then we'll work out where to find that box," said Beth, as she ran down the stairs. She slid the carefully iced birthday cake to one end of the table, so they had space to spread honey on slices of bread.

Aunt Jean was arranging fairy cakes on wooden platters. "That box you were asking about, Beth, is it important?"

"Yes, it might stop those crows becoming even more powerful."

"Then ask your Uncle Pete. I don't discuss magic with Aggie Sharpe. She and I have had too many arguments over the years, so we stick to safe topics like crochet and politics. But Pete often visits her farm to drink herbal tea and discuss plant lore and magical ethics. He might know about a box."

"Where is he?"

"Working with the pine that fell last week."

Beth finished her bread in three bites, then ran out the back door, followed by her friends.

"He's leaving a portion of the fallen pine to encourage new life in the woods," she explained as she led them through the trees, "and harvesting the rest for heat and light and craft."

The **THUNK THUNK THUNK** of an axe guided them across the woods to the tall wrinkled old man.

"Uncle Pete! Do you know of a box with links to Mrs Sharpe or the crows or the Promise Keeper?"

He frowned and aimed the blade at a branch jutting up from the fallen trunk. "I wonder if it's time for that box."

He chopped and the branch tumbled down.

Then he looked up at Beth. "The year you came to us, one of my oldest trees fell during the winter storms, and I was considering what I could create with the wood

I harvested. Aggie Sharpe said if I made a box, she would put it to very good use. So I made her a middling-sized box, of polished pine, with a subtle pattern of knot-holes on the lid, and invisible joins at the corners. My best work. Then the witch put something secret inside, locked it and hid it away. I haven't seen the box since." He sighed and swung the axe again.

"What secret did she put in it?" asked Molly. "Where did she hide it?"

"It's not hidden if you tell someone. And it's not secret if you share it. So I don't know. But I do know that the spell to hold it closed was so strong that it drained her. Aggie's tatties and onions were very poor that year and a bit straggly the year after. She said it was worth it because the box and its contents would be needed one day. And I know that it was an object the crows valued, that's why she took it and hid it. She's never liked crows."

Beth looked at her friends. "So we're searching for a beautiful pine box."

Theo leant forward and asked, "How do we open the box? How do we use what's inside?"

He leant back again fast as Uncle Pete swung the axe. "I don't know any of that, young man. Why not ask the old witch herself? She likes answering questions. That's why she runs all those workshops."

Beth thanked her uncle and they all turned to leave the woods. "If the box belongs to Mrs Sharpe," she said, "then we should start our search at Skene Mains Farm."

Uncle Pete shouted after them, "Be careful. It's not easy to find something hidden by a witch. And it's not wise to open it."

"Mrs Sharpe's farm has a lot of buildings and even more fields. Where should we search first?" asked Molly, as they crossed cold ridges of earth in the tattie fields they'd dug together last autumn.

"The farmhouse," said Atacama.

"Her house will be protected by witch's wards," said Innes.

"Therefore it's the most secure place on the farm," said Atacama. "The only place that isn't open to customers and workshop pupils. Theo, can you use your magic – very carefully – to get past her security?"

Theo shook his head.

"Can you talk us through it, then? Like you taught Molly to make a boundary?"

"Probably." He glanced round them all. "Beth, you contain lots of strong growth and healing magic. Innes, you're full of transformation magic, so if you can follow my instructions without arguing, you'll be fine. Atacama, sphinxes are connected to the same classical magic as my family, so you should be able to work simple spells. And Molly, you have all that latent magic from your witch ancestors."

"No, I don't!"

"Yes, you do. Remember when I used a revealing spell in the Keeper's Hall last year, and it showed that white light in your hand? That was your latent magic. It gets stronger every time you manipulate your curse. You're becoming a witch, Molly, whether you like it or not."

Beth stepped away from her.

"But I haven't chosen this, Beth! I don't want to be a witch!"

"You might have to choose it," said Innes, "if you're going to defeat that massive dog in magical combat. Just embrace it, Molly. Power is nothing to be afraid of."

Molly sighed. "Unless you're so powerful you can blow up the land you're standing on, like Theo."

Theo said, "You'd be a witch, not a magician, with access to less power, so less chance of causing harm with it."

"Witches cause harm all the time," said Beth. "A witch cursed my trees to burn. A witch cut us with those ice-blades on the moors. Mrs Sharpe's failure to guide Estelle properly led to the charged-up curses. Witches are dangerous. Witches are dark magic. Witches are..." She sighed, and looked at Molly. "Witches are everything that's wrong with the magical world. I can't be friends with a witch."

"I'm not a witch yet, Beth. I don't even know any magic spells!"

Innes laughed. "You can shift into a hare or a mouse at will. You can shift back by creating a boundary. That's magic, Molly. Those are spells. You already do magic spells."

"But I don't *choose* to do magic. I only do it when I have to."

Beth frowned. "All those races with Innes? All those times you shift to run somewhere faster or more easily? You already use magic for fun and for convenience."

Molly turned away and walked off towards the farm buildings, not sure how she should reply to Beth, and even less sure what she should do with Theo's revelation about the white light that had glowed between her fingers last autumn.

When they all reached the farmyard, Innes said, "My mum's been buying fruit and veg from Mrs Sharpe since I was a baby, and I've been in the shop, the bunkhouse, the sheds, the barns, the workshop, but never in the farmhouse."

"So that's the logical place for the box to be," insisted Atacama.

Theo said, "She has the house locked up tight."

"I could kick the door in," said Innes. "Please, let me kick the door in."

Theo shook his head. "It's locked up tight with magic. I can feel the witch's wards: the layers of spells protecting every door and every window, as well as the ground below the house and the air above. The front door could be wide open and there would be no safe way in unless she invited you. Her witch's wards will crash down on anyone who goes in uninvited."

"I could sneak in as a mouse," said Molly.

"Not this time. Nothing can get in." Theo sighed.

"Obviously, I could get in, if I didn't mind destroying the house and probably everyone within twenty miles. And if I wasn't so powerful, if I could use just a tenth of my stored energy, I could get in with no damage at all. But I can't. So I'll try to teach you all the safest way past witch's wards."

Beth said, "I'm a dryad, not a witch or a magician. I don't do magic spells. It's not right, it's not my role in the world."

Molly said, "I shouldn't really, either, should I? I'm just a girl, and a part-time hare, and a reluctant mouse. I'm not a proper magic-user. And of course, I don't want to be. I'll just watch."

"No," said Beth. "Watching will encourage them. Come on Molly, let's search the other buildings and find the box before they blow themselves or the house up."

Molly walked away from Theo explaining how to identify and separate strands of magic, and followed Beth towards the bunkhouse.

Beth found a key under a bucket by the door. "I'll search downstairs, you search upstairs."

Molly ran upstairs to the top-floor bedroom she and Beth had shared briefly last year. She looked out the window and saw the sphinx and the two boys standing three steps away from the back door of the farmhouse. Atacama was batting bright sparks of what must be magic between his paws. Innes and Theo were laughing.

Molly sighed, then looked under the beds. She found a balled-up pink sock, but no pine boxes.

She opened the wardrobe, which had the only door on the witch's property that creaked satisfyingly, and saw nothing but clothes hangers. She walked across the tiny landing to the room Innes and Atacama had shared. It was empty too, with a view of the cold hills in the distance.

The floor below had higher ceilings and more rooms, but contained nothing except beds, wardrobes and four months of dust.

She ran downstairs. Beth was teetering on a stool, looking in the highest kitchen cupboards.

"Nothing upstairs," said Molly.

"Nothing here either. Maybe Atacama's right and this is too public for something she wanted to hide. But I won't help them break into the house until we've searched everywhere else."

They checked sheds and barns, and found cobwebs and echoes. They checked the shop, and found one wrinkled brown apple and bare shelves.

As they left the shop, Molly glanced across at the boys. They weren't laughing now.

Atacama was lying on the ground, pinned down by a shimmering wall of light, which Innes was struggling to lift off him. Theo's hands were clenched behind his back, as he forced himself to stay away from the sphinx.

Molly ran towards them. "Do you need help?"

"Yes, please!" said Theo. "Innes has more muscle than magical sense, and I can't explain to him how to lift that shutter up."

"I can't hold it much longer," gasped Innes. "It's so heavy, it's going to crush him!"

Theo said, "But it's not *heavy*, that's the point. It's not weight, it's energy. You have to feel it differently, you have to treat it differently."

"All I can feel is something that's mangling my hands and flattening my friend!"

Molly said, "Let me."

She slid her hands between the flickers of light and the ribcage of the shaking sphinx. She felt Atacama's warm fur on the backs of her hands and the light's sparkling coolness on the palms.

Theo said, "It's not heavy, Molly. Don't use strength or force. That makes it defensive. Just ease it up."

Innes said, "Careful, don't—"

"Shut up, Innes!" snapped Theo. "Get out of the way and let Molly do it."

Innes flinched, but kept his voice steady. "Do you have it, Molly? Can you stop it crushing him?"

"Yes, I think so." The wall of light was playing gently on her palms and she was sure it was easy to persuade.

Innes took a deep breath and pulled his hands away.

Molly felt the pressure of the light increase. But it wasn't painful or heavy, just intense.

She heard Theo behind her. "Now I want you to—"

Molly said, "Yes, I know." She raised her hands and the light danced upwards, wafting like a silk scarf, lifting smoothly off the sphinx.

Innes dragged Atacama away.

Molly asked, "Will I keep lifting, or let it down now?"

Theo said, "Can you possibly lift it off the whole house? It's the final layer."

Molly gave the light a gentle push, and it floated over the roof and out of sight.

She turned round. "Is Atacama ok?"

Innes, Beth and Theo were staring at her.

"Is he ok?"

The sphinx sat up, nodded his thanks to Molly and began to wash his ears.

"Are *you* ok?" said Innes. "That was too heavy for me. But you just—"

"I'm fine. You probably did most of the hard work, Innes, I just gave it one last little shove." She didn't look at Beth.

As Theo, Atacama and Beth walked into the house, Molly grabbed Innes's left arm and pulled his hand towards her. She saw red and purple marks across his palm. Burns and bruises. She showed him her hands. They were unmarked.

"That felt completely natural. As natural as being a hare. Considerably more natural than being a caterpillar. But Beth... Beth says she can't be friends with a witch."

"If Beth wants to be your friend, she has to be friends with who you are. And she's almost forgiven me for cursing my dad. She still hassles me about it, obviously, but she has to keep talking to me, in order to hassle me. She's a tree and they're not as flexible as water." He smiled at her. "We have a box to find, an army to defeat and a Keeper to stop. Once we've done all that, we can worry about the really difficult stuff, like Beth's attitude to magic."

And they walked into the witch's house.

Chapter
Twenty-two

Molly and Innes followed their friends through the unlocked door, into a big entrance hall floored with black and red tiles.

"Let's fetch all Mrs Sharpe's wooden boxes," said Innes.

"The box we want is smooth pine and has knotholes on the top," said Beth. "It'll be easy to recognise."

"Easy for you. The rest of us should just pick up *any* wooden container bigger than a hankie box and smaller than a coffin."

Innes and Theo ran upstairs; Beth, Molly and Atacama split the rooms downstairs.

Molly stepped into a room overflowing with books. Every shelf was filled with books, and the floor was covered with stacks of books. Some were brightly coloured modern novels, most were old and leather-bound. She glanced at the titles on the nearest shelf, and noticed the red spine of a book called *The Beginner's Guide to Curses*. Molly grinned. She could have written that herself.

She looked at the gleaming books beside it:

The Liar's Guide to Promises
The Musician's Guide to Silence
The Shapeshifter's Guide to Running Away
The Ninja's Guide to Knitting Patterns
The Writer's Guide to Spellchasing
The Magician's Guide to Circles and Tangents

At the very end of the shelf, she saw:

The Witch's Guide to Magical Combat

She pulled the book out, wondering if it would be more help against Mr Crottel than an exhibit from a tourist attraction, and flicked through it. Each page had a different spell written in blood-red letters at the top:

How to defeat with fire
How to defeat with ice
How to defeat with barbs and blades
How to crush your opponent with granite
How to bury your opponent for 1001 years
How to humiliate your opponent in seven simple steps

The pictures of combat and victory at the bottom of each page were small and faded, but when Molly peered closer at them, she could hear faint moans and screams.

She shivered, and decided that if she was going to defeat Mr Crottel in magical combat, she would win with her own skills, not with a witch's power, not with spells like these.

She closed the book and put it on the shelf. She turned her back on the guidebooks and looked round the room. The only wood she could see was the shelving, and there were no boxes.

She walked into the hall. Beth was standing in the doorway of the room opposite, shaking her head. "Lots of half-finished knitting, no pine boxes."

Atacama nudged a varnished wooden box through the kitchen doorway.

Beth said, "No, that's made of oak, can't you tell the difference?"

Innes and Theo came down the stairs, Innes with one big box in his arms, Theo with two smaller ones.

Innes's box was carved with the sinuous shapes of snakes and monkeys. Beth stroked it and shook her head. "That's an exotic wood, not native to Scotland."

Theo showed the two plain boxes he'd found. Beth shook her head again. "Far too old."

"Let's try the bunkhouse," said Innes. "There are lots of cupboards in the kitchen."

"Or the shop, with all those shelves," suggested Atacama.

"We've checked them already," said Molly. "There's just the classroom left."

They walked out of the witch's house, towards the barn

where they'd met last year, and pushed open the red door.

The barn was much colder than it had been in the autumn. Beth flicked the switch, and the lights came on with a buzz, dim and flickering, only illuminating the centre of the big classroom.

The room contained desks and chairs. No boxes.

Molly pointed at the row of cupboards built into one wall, each with words stencilled on the door:

KNIT YOUR OWN UNDERWEAR WORKSHOP SUPPLIES

TEABAG WORKSHOP SUPPLIES

CURSE-LIFTING WORKSHOP SUPPLIES

There were a dozen cupboards, each for a different workshop.

Beth opened the nearest one and lifted out balls of wool, bundles of knitting needles and a box of scissors.

Molly went straight to the curse-lifting cupboard.

"It can't be in there," said Innes. "We saw her open that cupboard to get maps and worksheets. We'd have noticed a box."

Molly flicked up the latch anyway, and saw shelves filled with scrolls, paper and pens. The bottom shelf was bending slightly under the weight of a piled-up metal chain.

Molly crouched down and looked more closely. The chain was wound round and round a pale wooden box.

"Beth, is this made of pine?"

Beth reached in and touched the smooth corner of the box, just visible past the loops of shining metal.

"Yes. This is a tree from my woods. It's Uncle Pete's work. We've found it..."

Molly carefully picked up the chained box and carried it to a desk.

They all stared at it. The box was tightly wrapped in layers of metal links. It would be impossible to lift the lid without removing the chain. And the chain was held together by a large silver padlock.

"We need the key." Molly turned to look in the cupboard.

"It's not in there," said a quiet voice from a shadowy corner at the back of the classroom.

Molly stood still as most of her friends surged past her towards the corner.

Innes dragged Snib into the light. Beth kicked her feet from under her and pushed her to the floor. Atacama crouched at her shoulder and bared his teeth.

Molly and Theo glanced at each other and walked towards the angry group gathered around the crow-girl.

Molly looked down at Snib. She was red-eyed, pink-nosed, white-cheeked and shaking.

Beth said, "Little sneak. Little spy. Little traitor."

"I am a sneak and a spy, I admit that. I'm about to be a traitor too, but not to you. I'm about to betray Corbie."

"But you were spying for Corbie," said Atacama.

"Yes. Because he'd have kept me in the ranks of his army if I hadn't agreed to spy for him. Spying on you gave me the chance to move around freely and find my own way to save the curse-hatched from Corbie's plans. I'm sorry that I had to tell him about the star iron, and about Theo's powerlessness, to keep his trust. But now I'm here, ready to do… what I've always known I have to do."

"Don't listen to her," said Innes. "She's convinced us once before. We can't fall for it again."

"Let's use that chain to tie her up and keep her out of the way," said Beth.

"Use that chain, against me?" Snib laughed, a weak panicky giggle. "You can't take the chain off the box without me. And you need to open the box, so you need me."

She sat up.

Beth put her black-booted foot on Snib's chest and shoved her back down. "Stay down, spy." Beth looked round at the circle of faces above the crow-girl. "What should we do with her?"

"Listen to her," said Molly. "Listen to what she has to say about the chain and the box, then make up our minds."

Theo nodded. "Tell us what you know, crow."

Snib said, "There's something locked in the box."

"We already know that," said Beth.

"Something vital to Corbie and his army."

"We know that too," said Atacama.

"Something that could defeat both Estelle and Corbie."

"Yeah, we worked that out as well," said Innes.

"If you know so much, do you know how to open the box?"

"Cut the chain?" said Innes.

"No. The chain will only break when the key is inserted and the padlock is opened. And the chain isn't just keeping the box closed; the chain is also the link between curses and crows. When the chain is unlocked, every single link will be broken and whatever is in the box will be set free."

"Do you know what's inside?" asked Molly.

"No, but I know it's sad and lonely. I know it's been even sadder and lonelier since last October, when you killed my mother and released the Keeper from her babyhood. And I know I'm the only one who can free it."

"Why you?" asked Theo.

Snib looked at the heavy boot on her chest, then looked up at Beth. "Can I move, just a little?"

Beth nodded.

Snib pulled up her sleeve to show the key on her arm. "The curse that keeps it trapped in the box is the curse that hatched me. The caster worded the magic so that when I break the curse, I also break the link between curses and crows, and free all my brothers and sisters. I just have to use the key to open the lock."

"But Snib, if you break your own curse, you'll die," said Molly.

"I know."

"She might not, actually," said Theo. "If the wider link between all curses and all curse-hatched breaks before the ending of her own specific curse can kill her, she might survive. But that link will only break because she's breaking her own curse. I wonder which breakage the curse arc will recognise first? It's an interesting magical conundrum..."

"It's not *interesting*," said Molly. "It's Snib's life. It's too much of a risk."

"It's a risk I have to take," said Snib. "Someone must stop Corbie and Estelle, and someone must break the link between the crows and the curses. That link to dark magic isn't our strength, it's our weakness. And I have the key to break it."

Beth shook her head. "That box contains something powerful. We can't let this treacherous snivelling crow anywhere near it."

"Surely we don't need her to open the box," said Innes. "There are plenty of tools on this farm; we can find a saw and cut the chain."

Molly said, "But Mrs Sharpe told me to 'ask the crow'. She wanted us to involve Snib. Mrs Sharpe set this magic up and we have to trust her."

Beth laughed. "Trust a witch?"

"Trust Mrs Sharpe, yes," said Atacama. "Trust Snib, no."

"I think we have to trust them both," said Molly.

"We don't have time to argue," said Snib. "I have to do this right now. The Promise Keeper is on her way to Stone Egg Wood. Corbie has invited her to a feast, and once she's there he will ask her to charge up the best curses to create the strongest curse-empowered monsters for his army. If she agrees, he'll hide the star iron far from her, to keep her safe. If she refuses, if she wants to keep charging up curses that amuse her rather than useful ones, he'll threaten her with the star iron. He'll use it to control her and all her power. So there's no time to debate. Let me up, let me open the box, let me free whatever's inside."

"What if this crow is still working for Corbie?" said Beth. "What if she frees something that attacks us?"

"She's risking death by unlocking the chain," said Molly. "She's taking a much bigger risk than we are. If you're all scared of what's in the box, you can wait at a safe distance, and I'll stay here with Snib." Molly looked at Beth. "Though if you stay, your healing powers might help her recover after she breaks her own curse."

Beth shrugged, and lifted her boot from the crow-girl's chest.

"No," said Snib. "Don't waste time on me. I will either fall when the curse that hatched me breaks, or the link will sever in time to save me. I don't know which, but I do know there's no time to waste."

She sat up, then stood up.

"When I've unlocked the chain, please take whatever is in the box and get to Stone Egg Wood *fast*. That's why I waited here. I knew that whoever was clever enough to work out where the box was and why it was important, might also be clever enough to use what's inside to defeat Corbie and the Keeper. And I needed you to arrive before I opened the box, so that if this is the end of me, you can use the contents to stop Corbie's plans. So please Molly, please all of you, promise that you won't waste a moment on me. Promise that you'll leave me here, to die or recover, on my own."

Molly looked at Snib's tear-filled eyes and shaking hands. She thought about the courage it would take for Snib to break the curse that had hatched her, the curse that kept her alive. Molly had to give Snib whatever she needed right now.

So Molly said, "Yes, I promise."

Theo frowned at her, but Molly nodded at him. Theo said, "I promise too."

Innes shrugged. "Ok. I promise."

Atacama said, "I promise."

Beth nodded too. "Easy done. I promise not to waste a minute on you."

Snib smiled but Molly saw that her hands were trembling even more. Maybe she hadn't wanted them to make that promise after all.

Snib walked towards the chain-wrapped box. She pulled off her ripped cardigan, to reveal her thin bare arms. One covered in pale bruises from her fall, the other with a long key-shape shining like a burn from wrist to elbow.

Theo asked eagerly, "Is the curse image coded into your skin? How do you take it off to use it?"

"I don't take it off. It's part of me. I am the key."

"How do you *know* all this? Is it written down in a book of curses, or are you told as you grow, or—?"

"I just know it. Our curses bring us out of the eggs,

so they're part of us. I've woken every morning feeling the loneliness of whatever is trapped in this box; I've gone to sleep every night knowing I'm a prisoner of this curse too. Now I'm going to free my curse victim, and break the link between my family and curses forever."

She lifted the silver padlock with her left hand, and pushed her right index finger into the keyhole.

The key on her arm glowed.

The padlock opened and the chain started to break.

One by one, the links started to crack, to shatter, to explode. The chain slipped from the box and fell to the floor in a heavy rain of broken metal ovals.

As the weight of the chains slid away, the box lid began to rise.

As the box lid rose, Snib fell.

With the padlock in her hand, she slid to the floor, among the fractured links. The key on her arm flared brightly, then faded away.

Snib sighed, then her eyes closed.

Chapter Twenty-three

Molly knelt beside Snib, among the fallen links, which were still cracking and popping like seeds under a grill. Had Snib broken her own link fast enough to save her life?

Molly put her hand on the crow-girl's throat. She couldn't feel a pulse, though she wasn't sure if she was feeling in the right place.

Molly looked up. "Come on! Help her."

"No," said Innes. "We promised not to. We must use what's in the box, right now. That's what we promised to do."

"Don't be daft," said Molly. "That wasn't a promise I ever intended to keep."

She felt a tiny tremor under her hand. "She's not dead yet. Beth, come here. You're a healer."

"A healer of trees, not a healer of crows. Or spies. Or traitors."

Molly stared at Beth. "You talk about dark magic and how bad it is, but I don't think magic is dark or light, good or bad. It's what you do with magic that counts. So get down here, on the floor, and do some good with your magic, Beth. Use whatever you have to save this girl. Now!"

Beth flushed and knelt beside Molly. She ran her hand down Snib's body, and shook her head. "I can feel the life leaving her – much faster than it ever leaves a tree. But I can't help her. It's not like a broken branch or even a broken bone. I don't have enough power."

Molly frowned. "Theo, you have plenty of power. You and Beth could save her together, like you once joined mosaic fragments together, couldn't you?"

Theo stepped away. "I have too much power. I can't save her, I'd kill her and everyone else here."

"Then just use a bit of your power, just one hair's worth."

"It doesn't work like that. When I open up to the magic, I get it all. And I can't control the quantity and strength of the power stored in my newly grown hair."

"There must be a way to reduce the power you have!" Molly turned away from the dying crow-girl and saw the balls of wool in the corner.

She jumped up. "I have an idea. Beth, keep her alive. Think of her like a sapling. Innes, Atacama, sit Theo down in a chair and don't let him get up."

But no one did anything, everyone just stared at her, as she ran over to the **KNIT YOUR OWN UNDERWEAR** cupboard and grabbed a pair of scissors.

She ran back and shoved Theo into the nearest chair, so he didn't tower over her. "Hold still."

She grabbed a handful of black hair above his left ear and cut it off.

"Hey!" He jerked away.

"Stay still! Or I'll take off an ear too."

She cut more hair away, from above and behind his ear. She tried to be careful, gentle and precise. But she also tried to remove lots of hair as fast as possible, so it was extremely untidy, and she nicked his skin occasionally.

Molly muttered, "You have too much hair, too new, too thick, too strong, storing too much power. So, less hair means less power and safer magic. Yes?"

Theo whispered, "I'm not sure it will work like that. And I'm going to look awful!"

She moved round to the other side. Theo was sitting very still. As she chopped off more hair, Molly said, "Even if it doesn't work, your hair will grow back. But this is Snib's only chance. Beth, how is she?"

"Fading away."

Molly stepped back. Theo's feet were haloed with a ring of shiny hair. His head was spiky with hacked hair on both sides, but a narrow line of smooth untouched hair ran from above his forehead to the nape of his neck, like a horse's mane.

"Right. That's about one tenth of the hair you had before. Can you control that amount of power?"

Theo held his palms close together. A spark danced between them.

He grinned. "Yes!"

He scuffed through the circle of his own hair, ran to Beth and grabbed her hand. "Guide me. You understand life and cells. I work with atoms and energy. If you slow me down and keep me gentle, together we can save her."

They knelt, Theo's left hand and Beth's right hand on Snib's shoulders, their other hands joined above her heart.

Beth said, "Careful, careful," then, "Slow down, those twigs are delicate."

Theo laughed. "They're not twigs, but I see what you mean."

As Molly watched, a tinge of colour returned to Snib's face, then her ribcage rose in a sudden gasp of breath.

Beth let go of Theo's hand and backed away, banging into a desk. She looked at Molly. "Thank you for making me do that. I can't believe I thought I had the right to refuse. I can't believe I nearly didn't even try."

"I can't thank you sincerely until I've looked in a mirror..." said Theo.

"So can you use your power now?" said Molly. "Not just for this, but to defend yourself?"

He smiled. "Yes. I can control it, so I can use it. I should have thought of cutting my hair before!"

"You didn't think of it," said Atacama, "because it's made you look ridiculous."

Innes grinned. "Oh, I don't know. It's got a sort of ancient warrior look to it..."

"Is she ok?" asked Molly. The crow-girl was breathing normally, though her eyes were still closed.

"She's fine," said Theo. "She's alive and she's free of the link to her curse. She might sleep for a while."

"Now that we've kept her alive, but broken our promise to her," said Innes, "let's not make her bravery pointless. Let's look in this box."

The lid had risen a little, but they couldn't see inside. Innes eased it all the way up. The flickering glow from the classroom's fluorescent light shone on a white bird. A small skinny awkward white bird sprawled across the inside of the box.

"Is it dead?" Beth reached out to pick it up.

The bird jerked away from her hand and squawked weakly.

Under the bird, they saw fragments of white stone eggshell.

"It's a curse-hatched," said Theo.

"It's not a crow," said Atacama. "It's not black."

"It's an albino crow," said Beth. "Look at its pink eyes."

"No wonder it was lonely, locked in a box with just its shell for company. How did it survive all those years?" asked Molly.

"We live on the power of our curses," said Snib. "We don't need to eat or drink, if our curse is strong."

They looked round. Snib was sitting up, rubbing her arms. "You broke your promise to me. You didn't leave me."

"We never meant to keep the promise," said Molly. "How could we leave you? Sorry I lied, but you said we didn't have time to debate, so I just agreed."

She helped Snib up. "Are you ok?"

"I think so. It feels strange, not being weighed down by a heavy curse."

Snib lifted the little white bird out of the box. It snuggled into her hands and its right wing flopped open, showing the image of a pale flame glimmering on its feathers.

"Why did Mrs Sharpe lock this bird in a box?" asked Molly.

"Because witches do dark cruel things," muttered Beth.

"No, I think Mrs Sharpe had a very good reason. Look," Theo pointed at rows of tiny lines and triangles carved on the inside of the shell shards. "The bird has written her story."

He used a fingertip to turn the delicate pieces of shell.

"This bird was inside the stone egg for centuries. She absorbed all the time that was burnt off the baby Promise Keeper, when Nan was keeping Estelle artificially young. Then she hatched when we stopped Nan's nightly ceremony."

Innes said, "Those shapes aren't words."

"Yes, they are. This is cuneiform, one of the earliest forms of writing, and fairly easy to do with a beak. The bird's story says she contains all the time, learning and wisdom Estelle was never allowed." He looked up, his eyes bright under his vicious hairstyle. "So that's why Mrs Sharpe wanted us to find this bird! We don't need to attack Estelle with the star iron. We need to give her this bird, to reunite her with her lost self: with all the growth her mind and character should have achieved along with her body. Instead of making her weaker, we need to make her stronger."

Atacama said, "Is that sensible?"

"Reuniting her with the wisdom trapped in this bird will add to her power, but it should also make her less likely to misuse that power. Let's get this bird to Stone Egg Wood, before Estelle starts to charge up curses for Corbie's army rather than her own entertainment."

"What's our plan of attack?" asked Innes.

"We don't need a plan of attack now – we have my power..." Theo shrugged and tried to look modest. "If Corbie won't let me near her, I can probably destroy his little curse army. If the Promise Keeper resists taking this bird in her hand, I can probably force her. But I'll do less damage with all of you there to keep the army out of my way, and to help me persuade Estelle rather than fight her. Who wants to come with me?"

"I'll come," said Innes. "To back you up and because I can't keep running from my dad."

"I'll come," said Molly. "To rescue all those curse victims and to face Mr Crottel."

Atacama nodded. "I'd rather guard all of you, than guard the back door of a sweetie shop."

Beth said, "I can't come inside the wood, because the fossilised trees would turn me to stone, but I'll stand sentry outside."

Snib said, "I'll come as well, to stop Corbie using my brothers and sisters as his soldiers, and to keep them out of the way of Theo's attack."

"So let's all go to Stone Egg Wood," said Theo.

"How?" asked Molly. "We've lost the bikes, walking will take too long, and we can't all fit on Innes's back."

Theo smiled. "Let me organise transport."

He scooped the drifts of hair up from the floor. "Never leave loose magic lying around."

They walked out into the farmyard.

"Before we go, let's put those witch's wards back." Theo flicked a finger and the shimmery curtain slid over the roof to surround the house again.

Then he waved his hands and a tissue of woven light emerged from the ground beneath their feet. They all rose a hands-breadth into the air.

"A flying carpet," announced Theo.

"But we're not standing on anything solid," said Innes. "We're only standing on light."

"*Only* on light? This is pure energy. This is real strength and power. But I can conjure the image of a woolly rug if that would make you happier."

Theo bent down and touched the edge of the see-through fabric, and it became an opaque red-and-gold pattern of fruit and leaves.

They sat cross-legged on the soft, fluffy, entirely non-existent carpet.

And they flew over the moors, towards the wood

where the rogue Promise Keeper and the curse army were gathering for a feast.

The ground far below was racing by at dizzying speed, so Molly decided to focus on something closer. She looked at the albino bird nestled in Snib's hands.

"Will re-uniting this bird with Estelle hurt the bird?"

Theo said, "No, we'll be reuniting Estelle with her lost years, bringing together two things that were ripped apart. It will be right for the bird, not wrong."

Molly stroked the crow's white head. She thought of the fluffy baby bird that she'd met last year, and the hare on his wing. Mickle, her own curse-hatched. "Have we harmed the curse-hatched, by breaking their links to the curses?"

"Absolutely not," said Snib. "I feel much happier now I'm not tied to a curse. I'm sure all my brothers and sisters feel better too, but they probably don't realise why. Once I tell them they're free of curses forever, they might refuse to fight in Corbie's army."

"But he'll still have all those curse-casters and curse-charged monsters," said Innes. "And my dad. And Molly's green dog."

Beth looked at Molly. "You can now lift your curse without harming Snib's brother. And we know where Mr Crottel is. So how are you going to tackle him?"

Atacama said, "To break her curse, Molly must defeat the caster herself, in magical combat."

"Or I could just ask him nicely," said Molly.

Even Beth laughed at that.

"You've tried everything else," said Innes. "It's time to use magic and win in combat."

"I can't do that," said Molly. "I'm not a witch."

Theo said, "Not yet, but you're close. You have significant latent ability, enhanced by your expert manipulation of your curse and swift learning of boundary spells. You can become a strong witch, Molly. We don't have much time before you meet your curse-caster again, so you'd have to skip the beginner's guide to sparkly magic and go straight to the aggressive spells. I could teach you a few combat spells right now."

Molly sighed. "I'd prefer to defeat him as myself, not as a witch."

Innes said, "But Mr Crottel is a witch in his human form and a massive fanged deephound in his dog form. How can you possibly fight him, either as a girl or a hare? Or even as a goat or deer or anything else you've shifted into? You have to become a witch."

Molly glanced at Beth.

The dryad grasped Molly's hand. "You know I don't want you to stay cursed, and I also don't want you to choose this dark way to break your curse. I can't decide which is worse. But... I'm your friend, Molly, and I'll try to understand whatever you do."

Molly squeezed Beth's hand, then said quietly, "So, Theo, if I wanted to, how would I...?"

Theo smiled. "You already have plenty of magic you can use as a weapon. Think about the way you feel when you choose to become a hare, the way you feel when you place your power into a line, the way you felt when you knew exactly how to lift that witch's ward off Atacama. I can teach you to use that magic to fight, to attack, to hurt, to destroy."

Molly frowned at Theo. "To hurt? To destroy?"

He shrugged. "It's magical combat. It's not gentle or polite. I can show you how to grasp the magic within your reach and become a witch to defeat your curse-caster. But only if you want to, Molly. It's your choice."

Molly looked round at everyone sitting on the flying carpet. They were all staring at her.

This was her chance to choose. Not just whether and how to break her curse, but who and what she wanted to be. It was her choice...

Chapter
Twenty-four

Molly remembered the pictures in *The Witch's Guide to Magical Combat* and the faint noises of pain and fear she'd heard from the pages. She thought about Mrs Sharpe tangled in her own knitting curse. She thought about Beth's wood, burnt and blighted by Molly's own ancestor.

She looked at all her friends, sitting round her on the flying carpet, and she shook her head.

"I don't want to be a witch. I've never felt like a witch. I feel like a hare, and I'm getting quite used to my mouse form, but I've never once felt like a witch. It seems daft to become something that I'm not, in order to stop being something that I am."

"We can't let you fight a deephound as a hare or a mouse," said Innes. "Please let Theo teach you a fighting spell."

"I probably don't need spells. I have this." She took out the collar.

Innes jerked away. "What *is* that? It feels cold and sharp and sickening." He shivered. "It feels like the bridles humans used to make for enslaving kelpies."

"Sorry." She shoved it back in her pocket. "I found it in the cabinet of curiosities. The label said it could control a faery dog, and, Atacama, you said deephounds were also called faery dogs, so do you think it will work on Mr Crottel?"

Atacama nodded. "Oh yes. If you can pin down a monstrous dog on your own, and buckle that nasty artefact round his neck, then it will work. But I'm not sure how you'd manage all that without one of Theo's spells."

"We're nearly there," said Theo. "Do you want a quick guide to magical combat before we go in?"

Molly said firmly, "No thanks."

The carpet floated down, then faded into the ground, and they were all sitting cross-legged on icy heather.

Theo stood up and unzipped the borrowed grey fleece. It turned into a golden linen cloak, over a gleaming white tunic. He smiled. "At least one of us should be dressed for a feast."

They walked into a low peaty tunnel. Snib led the way, with Theo behind her and the rest straggling in a line after them. The dim air in the tunnel was warmer than the bright winter air outside.

Snib stopped at a curve in the tunnel and retreated two paces, setting off a domino reaction of squashed toes and banged noses. She whispered, "There are guards, but not proper crow guards. Those little squashy things."

Beth pushed past and peered round the corner. "Manky, Minging and Mawkit." She sighed. "They've given up the beauty of my living wood to be bouncers at the doors of Corbie's fossilised Stone Egg Wood."

Theo said, "I'll deal with them."

"No, don't hurt them," said Beth. "I want them to come home safe, because their fungus is part of our life cycle. Let me get them away from Corbie's influence, before they do anything else dark, dangerous or daft."

Beth stepped round the corner. "Greetings Manky, Minging and Mawkit."

"She's always politer to monsters than to her own friends," muttered Innes.

Beth smiled. "I invite the three of you to return home."

"We are home. We have new jobs here. Corbie promised that when his curse army destroy their enemies, his crows will get the eyes and our fungi will get the rest."

"Corbie's army won't last long enough to destroy anyone, because you will let my friends through," Beth waved the others to stand behind her, "and they will defeat the crows, then you will return to the leaf litter and fallen trees of our shared home."

Molly saw the three small grey figures, with their plump arms folded, standing in front of the carved wooden doors. The fungus fairies looked lumpy and badly put together compared to the smooth shapes of the curving trees and writhing curse-victims cut into the doors.

"No," said Manky. "We're on guard and we won't let anyone through. If you try to break in, we'll warn Lord Corbie and he'll—"

"Lord Corbie!" said Snib. "That's ridiculous."

"He'll send out his charged-up curse monsters. We've seen them all, because we've been in charge of letting in the new recruits. But we can't let you in, Beth of the Birches. You don't smell of curses."

"I'm not going in. But my friends are. The crow lives here. The girl is a curse victim. The kelpie cast a curse last year. The sphinx has just recovered from a curse. And the magician is a regular and unrepentant curse-caster. They'd all fit in fine with Corbie's curse army."

Manky shook his head. "They don't stink of curses, like those curse-empowered monsters inside. And we know you're not friends with His Crowship. So we won't open the doors."

"Fine. I can open them," said Snib.

"So can I," said Innes.

"See, you don't even need to open the doors," said Beth. "Just step out of the way, then get back to work in the woods, where you belong."

"No," said Manky. "You can't boss us around any more. You've never offered us any kind of power, any kind of excitement."

Beth smiled again. "My family and my trees have offered you the chance to be part of a living growing ecosystem, and if that isn't exciting, I don't know what is."

"So that's how dryads define excitement," Innes muttered to Molly. "Watching plants grow slowly upwards! That explains a lot."

Beth continued, "But I don't have to offer you anything. I can just do this…" She leant over the heads of the fungus fairies and laid her hands on the wooden doors.

And the carvings reached out for the fungus fairies. The trees on the doors stretched, their branches lengthened and their twigs reached for Manky, Minging and Mawkit.

The three fairies leapt out of the way and Manky flung his arms in the air. A pale frenzy of mushrooms burst from the peat floor, walls and ceiling. All growing towards Beth, covering her feet, dropping onto her hair.

Beth laughed. "I'm not afraid of anything from the earth. That's where my life comes from too." She moved gently away from the fungi at her feet, carefully brushed the fungi off her head, then snapped her fingers.

Roots shot out of the earth. Long thin snaky dirt-covered roots. Living roots of the stunted trees growing above and dried roots of the trees which had grown on the moor centuries ago.

The fungus fairies squealed and ran, but Beth's friends stood in a solid line across the narrow tunnel, blocking their escape. The roots wrapped round the fairies, like hoops round a barrel. Then the roots pulled the three fairies back towards the doors, where the carved trees bent down, lifted them up and hugged them hard to the planks.

Beth said calmly, "Now my friends will go in. And you three will stay out here with me and discuss the nitrogen cycle."

Snib walked forward, whispered to a carved wooden bird in a carved wooden tree, and the doors opened wide.

Molly saw Corbie's curse army, sitting down to lunch.

Last time Molly had been here, Stone Egg Wood had been quiet. Apart from crows roosting in the highest branches and fledglings dozing in nests lower down, there had been nothing in this underground wood but tall pale-grey stone trees.

Now the place was bright and bustling.

Through the pillar-like trees, in the light of silvery lanterns, she could see a long table set up in the clearing in the middle of the woods.

She could see birds perched on branches of the surrounding trees and birds circling high in the air under the far-away ceiling.

Around the table she saw trolls, mermaids and monsters. She saw the two boys from the screen at the Hall, calmly spitting out insects and stones. She saw a fiery sheep, a fanged goat, and a white dog with red ears and starry eyes. She saw a man with his own rain cloud and the weeping thistle girl. She saw tiny flying snakes and huge horned wyrms. She saw a minotaur and a miniature dragon. She saw a tiny fairy in a daffodil-yellow dress, sitting on a stone twig.

Beyond the new recruits, Molly saw smaller tables

covered in jugs and bowls, and beyond those was a large pool of water.

Theo led Molly, Innes, Atacama and Snib cautiously towards the feast, walking in the dim shadows by the peaty wall.

At the distant top of the long table, they could see Corbie in a high black throne, with Estelle seated in a lower gold throne on his right and Mrs Sharpe in an even lower grey chair on his left.

Mrs Sharpe was wrapped in her own tangled knitting.

Corbie was bright-eyed and happy, talking loudly and laughing louder.

Estelle was happy too. She had dozens of mirrors from the Chamber of Promises piled on the table beside her goblet, and she was picking them up to admire her reflection, while laughing at Corbie's jokes.

Theo held up his hand and whispered, "This won't be as easy as I'd hoped. Let's try to get close to Estelle and hand her the bird without getting into a fight."

Innes raised his eyebrows. "I thought your awesome power could handle anything. Are you doubting yourself now?"

Theo shrugged. "There are five times as many curse-enhanced beasts here as we saw on the moor. And I can feel immense amounts of power from Estelle. Look how weak the white crow is. This bird has all the wisdom from the lost years; Estelle has all the strength. Estelle is the most powerful Keeper I've ever seen. I could probably beat her, but there would be a lot of collateral damage. To these trees. To the crows. To the curse-casters and curse victims. To you. I'd like to avoid a fight. But if we have to fight, this is what we do."

They all leant in close, as Theo murmured, "Innes and Atacama, you clear our path to the Keeper. Snib, undermine Corbie's hold over your brothers and sisters, keep them out of the fight, or, even better, bring them in on our side. Molly, keep the white crow safe, and do whatever is necessary to place her in Estelle's hands."

Everyone nodded, then kept walking quietly beside the peaty wall.

There was a rustling above them. Molly glanced up. A small brown-black crow was staring down.

Snib said, "Shhh, Gretta! Please!"

But the bird started to flap her wings noisily.

And everyone at the long table turned to look straight at them.

Chapter
Twenty-five

Theo sighed. "We'll have to do this the hard way." He stepped out into the light.

Molly looked over at the feasting table. She saw the boy with the wolf's head, a lion with a mane of tiny snakes, and several wyrms. There were lots of predators at the feast, and Molly knew that as soon as one of them made a sound she would shift into their prey. Then she wouldn't be able to give the bird to Estelle.

She grabbed a handful of moss from the base of the wall, squashed it into two plugs and shoved them into her ears. The damp fibres expanded and sealed her ears, cutting out all the sound around her, just as Theo called to Estelle, "Esteemed Promise Keeper, I greet you—"

Theo moved forward, with Innes on one side of him and Atacama on the other.

Snib tapped Molly on the arm and handed her the small white bird.

Molly couldn't hear anything, but as she followed her

friends, she could feel the faint fast beat of the bird's heart against her fingers.

Corbie stood up and started yelling. The beasts at the table opened their mouths, showing their fangs and tongues. Molly felt the ground under her feet vibrate with the noise, but she couldn't hear it, so it didn't trigger her curse. She was still human and she still held the bird safe in her hands.

Snib was no longer beside her. The crow-girl was scrambling expertly up the nearest tree.

Ahead of Molly, Theo was still speaking, holding his hands out towards Estelle, with Innes and Atacama walking protectively beside him.

Corbie leapt up onto the table, scattering the mirrors. Estelle frowned at him. Corbie pointed at one of the recruits at the bottom end of the table, then pointed at the group walking towards the feast.

The curse-army soldier stood up.

It was Innes's father.

Corbie stamped his foot on the table and the tall kelpie, his face scarred and angry, strode towards Innes.

Theo turned to Innes, and they spoke briefly. Innes smiled at Theo, nodded, then stepped forward to meet his father.

Molly didn't know what the boys had said to each other, but she could see the growing tension in Innes's shoulders as he walked towards his dad.

Corbie was patting his hands down into the air,

calming the rest of his army. Maybe he thought one adult kelpie would be enough to stop them getting to Estelle. Maybe he didn't realise what Theo's brutal new hairstyle meant.

But Molly knew that even though Theo's power could knock Mr Milne all the way back to Craigvenie, Innes had to deal with his father himself.

Innes and his dad met between two tall stone trees. Mr Milne pointed to his own ripped boots. Molly wondered if he was asking Innes to kneel, to grovel.

Innes shook his head. His dad leapt at him, grabbed his shoulders and threw him to the ground.

But it wasn't a boy who hit the ground, it was a horse. A large, thrashing, angry white horse.

Suddenly there were two horses.

The two stallions started to fight. Slashing with sharp hooves, biting with long teeth, barging with heavy shoulders, butting with bony heads and kicking again and again and again.

Theo walked past the horse fight, still talking to Estelle, who had her head turned away, checking her eye makeup in a glowing mother-of-pearl mirror.

Molly glanced round. Snib was balanced on a narrow branch, talking to a growing flock of crows, eagles, vultures and other black birds in the trees around her, their heads tipped and eyes bright as they listened.

Molly ran forward, ducking under a vicious kick from Innes, to join Theo. Her job was to get this bird into the

Promise Keeper's hands. She couldn't be distracted by concern for her friends.

She walked on one side of Theo; Atacama walked on the other.

Corbie was yelling again, this time at the flock of birds gathered round Snib.

The Keeper turned to Mrs Sharpe, who was trying to drink from a goblet, though her hands were tangled in muddy brown and yellow wool. Estelle prodded Mrs Sharpe, gestured towards Theo, then looked back down at her mirrors.

Theo glanced at Atacama, who nodded.

The witch struggled to her feet, her woollen bonds loosening just enough for her to move. Estelle grabbed a loose end of yellow wool, and looped it round the arm of her throne.

Innes and his father galloped past in their horse forms, biting at each other's ears and withers. When they reached the pool beyond the tables, they both shifted to human form, and began wrestling and punching. Molly could see a black eye blooming on Innes's face.

Both kelpies toppled into the water.

Mrs Sharpe wriggled and the windings of wool loosened even more, still tight round her neck, but flapping round her shoulders and arms, like a badly made cloak. The witch glanced at Estelle, then moved towards Theo, Molly and Atacama.

Atacama ran ahead to intercept her.

Even wrapped in her mossy silence, Molly was aware of a disturbance in the air above: falling feathers, whirling wings, slashing talons. She saw two flocks of birds wheeling overhead. Birds still loyal to Corbie and birds now persuaded to work with Snib were fighting each other high above the trees.

Then Molly looked from the treetops to the water far ahead of her. She saw a long pale-green tentacle rising out of the pool. The kelpies were fighting in their monstrous underwater forms.

Beside her, Theo was walking forward in a slow formal dignified approach to the top of the table. No one was blocking his way, because many of the birds who'd been listening to Snib were now circling the table, preventing the curse army recruits getting up from their chairs.

Molly saw fluffy fledgling crows mobbing the weather-witch who'd created the ice-ambush on the moor. The two boys with the beetles and gems were clutching each other under the table. And Mr Crottel was hiding his face in his paws, while black hawks dived towards him.

But as she watched, Corbie's birds fought back. They attacked Snib's birds, distracting and disrupting them so that Corbie's loyal soldiers could start to push through the wall of fighting birds.

The first to break through was a tall figure made of triangles of silvered glass. It sliced through the air towards Theo and Molly.

Theo flicked a hand, and the thousands of fragments

melted together, forming one solid mirror shape that toppled forward inelegantly.

Then Molly felt a gust of warm wind. The roc was swooping towards them, its broad wings shattering the trees in its way. Huge branches hit the ground with thumps Molly could feel in her heels.

The roc flew lower, and everyone still seated at the feast, no matter what side they were on, ducked under the table.

Molly couldn't hear the roc scream, but she could feel the rush of air as the giant bird glided down, demolishing more trees as it came. She shivered as she saw long sharp black talons, strong enough to crush an elephant, swooping towards her.

Theo caught a delicate white twig as it fell from a broken tree, and placed it on the tip of his index finger. The twig started to spin, faster and faster, like a tiny propeller. Theo blew gently and the spinning twig rose up into the air.

As it rose, still spinning, the twig grew and grew: branch-sized, then tree-sized. It created a strong whirlwind, knocking more nests from trees. The vortex of moving air caught the roc and threw it, like a frisbee, to the other side of the wood. The roc crashed to the ground, bringing down rows of trees and crushing two bikes up against the far wall. The roc lay there, in the distance, moving feebly. Still alive, but unable to attack again.

The soldiers crawled out from under the table, and tried again to shove past Snib's brothers and sisters.

Molly kept walking steadily forward, sidestepping the chaos around her.

She stepped over a russet egg rolling out of a broken nest. Now their link with the curses was broken, no birds would ever hatch from these stone eggs.

Ahead of her, Mrs Sharpe attacked Atacama. The witch knotted her cursed wool into nooses and nets, and threw them at the sphinx. Atacama attempted to leap over and round the traps, to tackle the witch.

Molly wondered why Mrs Sharpe, who had told them to search for the bird in the box, was now trying to stop them getting the bird to Estelle. Then Molly noticed the witch's glazed eyes, the wool still wrapped threateningly around her throat, and the glowing yellow fibres linking her to Estelle's throne. Maybe Mrs Sharpe wasn't free to make her own choices.

Mrs Sharpe was flinging nets of wool at Atacama, but more than half of her attacks landed nowhere near the sphinx. She was using large exaggerated gestures, her effort obvious to anyone watching her, but she wasn't aiming very accurately. Molly realised Mrs Sharpe was fighting the wool that was controlling her, as well as fighting the sphinx in front of her.

But enough of her wild woolly attacks were landing around Atacama's paws to trap him in tangled snares.

Molly turned to free Atacama from the wool. Theo grabbed her arm and pulled her forward. He mouthed something at her. She nodded. Her job was to take the bird to the Keeper, not to help her friends.

Snib was perched in the tree, surrounded by a blurred battle of the birds. Atacama was biting at mustard-coloured wool, struggling to get free. Innes was crawling in human form out of the pool, but was dragged back in by half a dozen thick tentacles.

Wyrms and wolves and waves of other curse-empowered creatures were now fighting their way from the long table, trying to attack Theo, trying to attack Molly.

Molly lifted one hand and touched the mossy earplugs, checking they were firmly in place. The noise of these angry predators wouldn't affect her, wouldn't shift her into their prey.

So she ignored them. She walked forward, the bird in her hands and silence in her ears.

Then she noticed the smooth fangs of a snake-maned lion and the curved claws of a heavy black wolf, and realised they could rip her apart in her human form too.

Corbie's soldiers were crashing against the wall of crows and hawks, swiping at wings and tails, knocking Snib's sisters and brothers out of the air.

If they all burst through, silence wouldn't protect Molly or the small bird she held from claws, teeth and anger…

Chapter Twenty-six

The curse army was breaking away from the feasting table. The wall of birds wasn't strong enough to stop them attacking Theo, Molly and the white crow.

Molly wondered what she could do to protect the small bird. She wondered what she could do to protect herself...

Then Theo stopped and faced the table. He lifted his hands and the thickest broken branches from the roc's descent rose up to create a pale knobbly fence behind the chairs at the feasting table, preventing any more guests getting up and joining the fight.

Theo resumed his steady walk towards Corbie and Estelle at the far end of the feast. Molly walked beside him, the battle still raging around her and above her.

Broken black feathers spiralled through the air, crumpled nests and crushed lanterns littered the ground.

Atacama and Mrs Sharpe were flinging claw strikes and nets of wool at each other.

Snib and Corbie were directing arrows of birds at each other.

Innes and his father were rising out of the water, throttling each other.

As she walked through the chaos, Molly knew Theo had been keeping the worst of it away from her and away from the bird in her hands.

But Theo would soon need all his power to defend himself. Because Estelle had finally put down the pearly mirror. She was no longer gazing at her reflection. She was staring straight at Theo.

And she looked angry.

Then the Promise Keeper stood up.

Theo gave Molly a gentle shove, so she took a couple of involuntary steps away from him. She banged into the legs of a boy who was spitting cockroaches at a vulture lifting him into the air. Molly backed out of the fluttering rain of insects and looked up at the boy struggling in the bird's grip.

She couldn't be sure which of them was on her side. But the boy was a victim of Estelle's charged-up curses, and the vulture had attacked her friends on the moor.

So she cradled the white bird in one hand, grabbed a skinny branch and jabbed it upwards into the splayed outer feathers of the flapping wing above her, hoping it would disrupt the vulture's flight.

The vulture jerked to one side, dropping the boy.

Molly spun away to protect the white crow from the boy's flailing feet as he fell, then turned back to help him up. The boy clamped one hand over his mouth, and used the other to give her a thumbs-up. She offered him the branch and he took it, then waved it threateningly at the vulture. Molly wrapped both hands round the bird again and looked round.

Estelle and Theo were now attacking each other with their full magical powers. Estelle was thrusting a wall of ice at Theo, who was slicing it up with a sword of fire.

All the curse-hatched and curse-army soldiers who were fighting in small groups began to move away from the unpredictable dangers of the elemental duel. Soon, Estelle and Theo had the centre of the wood to themselves.

But Molly couldn't move to safety. She had to edge round the magical combat and take the bird to the Keeper.

She sidled round the battle of fire and ice, trying to avoid the steam and sparks. The little bird in her hand flinched at noises Molly couldn't hear.

As the wall of ice melted away, Estelle conjured a wall of glass. Theo created a flaming hammer, and began to fracture the glass with repeated swings and blows.

Estelle was concentrating on blocking Theo's approach. She thought Theo was the threat. But the real threat to the Keeper was in Molly's hands, and Estelle wasn't defending herself against Molly.

Molly smiled, in her own silent world. She walked round the edge of the elemental duel. She needed to get behind Estelle while the Keeper was focused on Theo.

Suddenly her path was blocked by a tall curse-hatched woman, who bent down to seize a rusty axe from a dazed troll. The curse-hatched woman lifted the axe above her head and swung the wide blade straight towards Molly.

Molly ducked out of the way.

The woman lifted the axe again.

A soft black wing brushed Molly's shoulder as a young black eagle grabbed the handle of the axe.

The eagle jerked the axe from the woman's hands, flew upwards, and swung the axe so hard that it stuck into the trunk of the nearest tree.

The black eagle swooped back down to attack the tall woman, but she ran off. As the eagle somersaulted in a victory roll, Molly saw an image on the glossy feathers of his right wing. The image of a leaping hare.

Molly had just been saved by her own curse-hatched.

She nodded to Mickle, and he dipped his feathered head towards her.

Molly kept on edging her way round the magical combat. Now Estelle had created a waterfall, and Theo was slicing through it with a sharp rainbow. Theo was winning again. The bright flowing waterfall was becoming soggy grey drizzle.

Molly saw Estelle's mouth stretch wide in an angry scream. The Keeper picked up one of the glowing mirrors and ran her hand over it. Sparks flickered from the glass to her fingertips. She picked up another mirror and another, and drew sparks from each of them.

Molly looked behind her. The boy who'd been spitting cockroaches was standing still, his fingertips touching his open lips, his eyes confused. Nothing was crawling from his mouth.

Estelle was removing the extra power from the charged-up curses. That was exactly what they'd hoped for. But she wasn't drawing the energy back to save herself from the star iron, or because she was re-united with her lost wisdom. She was drawing the energy back to increase her own power, so she could defeat Theo.

Estelle lifted her hand and flung a trident of lightning. A three-pronged bolt of electricity flew towards Theo. He threw up a domed shield of light to deflect it, but the trident ripped through and struck him in the chest.

He fell hard to the ground.

Estelle threw half a dozen bolts of jagged lightning, which pinned him down and fenced him in, and suddenly Theo wasn't moving.

Molly wasn't moving either. She'd planned to creep up on a distracted Keeper in the middle of a fight, not walk towards a victorious one.

Molly looked round, to see if anyone could help her.

Innes had his tentacles wrapped round his father's human form and was slamming him on the ground by the pool.

Atacama was aiming a claw at the glowing wool connecting Mrs Sharpe to Estelle's throne.

Snib was riding on the back of a giant crow, swooping round a huge vulture that held Corbie in its claws.

Beth couldn't come past the door.

Theo was trapped by lightning.

Mickle, her own curse-hatched, was wrestling with another black eagle, both grasping each other's talons, pecking and flapping as they tumbled through the air.

No one could help her.

Molly took a breath. That was the only thing she could hear past the moss in her ears: her own breathing.

She glanced at the little bird in her hands. The white crow nodded at Molly, her eyes bright and her feathers smooth. She looked healthier and stronger than she had all day.

Molly walked towards Estelle.

Estelle looked at her. Molly kept walking. Estelle smiled, a thin cold smile, and mouthed something.

Molly shrugged and kept walking.

Estelle spoke again.

Molly held the small bird against her chest, the fingers of one hand curled to keep her hidden. Molly used her other hand to point to her own ears.

Estelle nodded. Suddenly, Molly and the Keeper were inside a bubble: a glistening bubble of warm scented air, big enough for them to stand in.

Molly looked at the Keeper, who covered her own ears, then pointed to the bubble. Was she telling Molly that this flimsy bubble would block out the noise of battle?

Molly looked past the swirling petrol colours at the squawking birds and roaring beasts on the other side of the thin soapy film. And she took a risk. She pulled the moss out of one ear.

She heard nothing.

The Battle of Stone Egg Wood was still raging outside

the bubble, but she couldn't hear it inside. Her shape-shifting wouldn't be triggered in here.

She pulled the moss from the other ear, as Estelle said, in the bored tone of someone asking a question for the third time, "I said: Why aren't you afraid of me?"

"I am," said Molly. "Very afraid. But I have a gift for you, so I hope you'll be kind to me."

"A gift?" Estelle's voice brightened. "Really! What?"

Molly held the small bird gently in both hands again, but her fingers curved and closed over the white feathers, so Estelle couldn't see what she was holding.

"It's something the crows were hiding from you. Their most precious object."

"Give it to me."

"I'll give it to you when you let Theo go."

They both glanced at the magician, trapped by barbed blades of lightning.

"I'll never let him go. He's too powerful and too persistent. Also that haircut is entirely inappropriate for a formal feast. Give me my gift anyway, hare-girl."

"No, I'll only give it to you if you let Theo go." Molly edged round the side of the bubble, like she was staying as far from Estelle as she could, but she held her hands in front of her, within reach of the Keeper.

She said, "This gift is rare and beautiful and no one else has one. I promise I'll give it to you, if you free my friend."

"I want it. And I'm not bargaining for it. Give it to me now."

"You can't have it, unless you let Theo go."

"I can have anything I want!" Estelle reached out, forced Molly's fingers open and grabbed the bird.

Now the Keeper held the white crow in her hands. The bird sat up, happy and gleaming, plump and beautiful, and flapped her wings. Estelle giggled.

The bird rose into the fragrant air and flew round Estelle's head.

Suddenly there was a blaze of light, as bright as all the sunrises in a century, all the sunsets in a millennium. When the flare of light faded, the bubble around them had lost all of its colour and most of its sheen.

The Keeper sighed. There was no bird in her hand or round her head. But her hands were moving gently like wings; her white cheeks had a wash of pink on them, like the pink of the bird's eyes; and there were lines around her own blue eyes – not makeup, but the gentle wrinkles that come from smiling and thinking.

Molly thought that the Keeper didn't look exactly like Estelle any more. She looked like Estelle's older sister or cousin: someone who walked confidently past mirrors rather than gazing at herself, someone who offered to help rather than laughing at someone in pain.

The Keeper looked at Molly. "Have I done something silly?"

Molly nodded. "But you can put it right—"

Then the bubble burst, the sounds of battle crashed in and Molly heard a dog bark.

Molly felt the usual body-shifting flash of heat in her bones, and she couldn't speak any more.

Chapter Twenty-seven

Molly stood on her hare's hind legs, so she could see the battle. But the battle had ended.

Innes was standing over his father, who was lying flat on the ground, his boots in the water.

Atacama and Mrs Sharpe were winding up the wool, side by side.

Snib was leaping from the giant crow's back to land beside Corbie, who was kneeling under the weight of the birds mobbing him.

Mickle was hovering protectively above his big sister.

Theo was sitting up, brushing sparks and ash from his golden cloak.

And the ex-soldiers of the curse army were rushing towards the doors, held open by Beth.

Molly saw a green dog, its fur matted and rot-coloured, slinking towards the exit.

Molly sprinted at top hare speed across Stone Egg Wood, leaping over fallen nests, spilled eggs, broken branches, bent feathers and ripped moss.

She chased after the deephound, following the exodus of monsters, many of whom were shrinking or becoming less monstrous as they ran. Estelle was already removing her energy from the remaining charged-up curses.

Molly realised that her own curse would be returning to normal, so the only animal she could be was this hare. She couldn't be a snake or a goat, and any half-formed plans she'd had about researching what ate dragons, so she could shift into something bigger and scarier than the deephound, were already out of date.

She could be a hare or a girl. Those were her only options for fighting the dog.

Or, of course, she could become a witch.

She remembered the violent pictures in *The Witch's Guide* on Mrs Sharpe's shelves. She heard Theo's voice in her head: *The way you feel when you choose to be a hare... use that to fight, to attack, to hurt, to destroy...*

She shook her head as she ran.

She wasn't a witch.

She was Molly Drummond: Edinburgh schoolgirl and part-time hare. And that's how she would defeat him.

She ran through the doorway and past Beth, who called after her, "Molly, be careful! Lifting your curse isn't worth losing your life."

Molly grinned as she ran out of the tunnel.

She was already past most of the curse-casters and curse victims. Molly saw two boys speaking to a warty troll, who was raising his hands in the same gesture Innes and Theo had used when they lifted curses. Perhaps the brothers would be completely free of their jewel and beetle curse now.

But she was past them already. Sprinting across the land, following the deephound, who hadn't taken the route across the burn towards Craigvenie. He was running deeper into the moor, towards the mountains massing on the horizon.

Molly chased after the huge green dog.

And she was faster than him. She wasn't shifting between hare and girl, as she had been when he'd chased her on the patchwork of farmland nearer town. This time, she was much faster.

She caught up with him less than a mile from the entrance to Stone Egg Wood.

The dog whirled round and bared his teeth.

Now Molly was alone, on the moor, with the creature who had cursed her. With his drool burning the heather, his fangs glinting in the winter sunlight, his claws gouging lines in the earth, and his flickering blue eyes staring right at her.

Molly didn't stop to worry about the speed and freedom she would lose if she defeated him and broke her curse. She knew she wanted Mr Crottel's malice out of her life. She wouldn't let any more of her choices be coloured by this witch's petty revenge.

So she leapt at him.

But it didn't work like a mouse jumping at a surprised cat.

The deephound snapped at her and she had to swivel in the air to avoid his teeth. She landed awkwardly and backed off.

Mr Crottel had seen her jump before. Leaping wasn't going to take him by surprise.

So Molly ran under him. She emerged under his stinking matted tail, and ran round him anti-clockwise.

He whirled after her, trying to snap her spine.

She turned on one paw, then ran clockwise. The dog whirled again to follow her.

Molly kept running round him, switching direction unpredictably. She used the ground beneath him too, darting under his belly, his chin and his tail.

The dog snarled and bit, and spun round trying to catch her.

She tried to keep close to his legs but ahead of his teeth, jerking and jinking, turning and leaping, sprinting round and round. The dog was howling and growling in frustration, as Molly kept out of reach of his crunching jaws and swinging drool.

She ran in tight circles, afraid of the massive dog, but also enjoying the power and precision of her hare body.

Then she felt a sudden heavy punch on her ribs, as she was swept sideways by the swipe of a huge green paw.

Molly was knocked off her four fast feet.

But she bounced back up and leapt away from the jaws that snapped in the air behind her.

And she kept on teasing the deephound. Careful now

of the paws as well as the teeth, she ducked and dived and dodged.

The hare ran rings around the dog.

Finally the dog began to slow. He was getting dizzy, his reactions becoming sluggish.

Molly jumped just a little further away and he leant over, trying to bite her in mid-air. But the dizzy dog leant too far, lost his balance, and toppled over.

Molly didn't hesitate. She found the longest scrape Mr Crottel had gouged in the earth as they faced off, she put perfect memories of running as a hare into it, she saw the earth before and the earth after, she leapt over…

And she landed as a girl.

With her clothes on. And her pockets. And everything in her pockets.

She unzipped her coat pocket, hauled out the collar, and threw herself at the dog. He leapt up, as she leapt at him.

She no longer had her speed or nimble paws. But she did have height and weight and hands.

So Molly clambered onto the giant dog's back, using her fingers to grip his fur and her knees to crush his ribs. She clung on as the deephound bucked and twisted, and just as she felt him take in a breath to snarl and turn her back to a vulnerable hare, she flung the collar round his neck.

The deephound stopped moving.

He stood still and quiet, shaking with fear.

Molly slid off him, holding onto both ends of the collar, then she stood beside him, smelling his sour breath and musky fur.

"I could fasten the buckle on this collar and have complete control over you. And the first order I would give you is: go back home, back to the deeps."

The green dog trembled.

"Or… I could take the collar off and you'd be free to live wherever you want. If I promise to take this collar off and put it back where I found it, far away from you, will you promise to lift my curse?"

The dog dipped and wagged his head, in a half nod.

"I don't trust you. I need your promise that you will lift my curse, completely and absolutely, with no limits or tricks. Or I will buckle this collar." She jerked the collar nearer his skin, and the deephound winced.

"Promise, now. And if you break your promise, I'll speak to my friend, the Promise Keeper…"

The dog nodded three times, carefully, but firmly.

Molly lifted the collar away slightly, holding it above the dog so the points of the nails were touching the hair of his neck.

The dog shifted, shaking off his mouldering fur then drawing it back in, and became an old man, with a greenish-grey suit and a green tie.

Mr Crottel ducked away from the collar. "You drive a hard bargain, girl. I'm not happy about it, but a promise is a promise, especially with a newly powerful Keeper."

He raised his hands. "I, Oliver Crottel of Deep End, lift my curse on Molly Drummond. Now, and forever."

He turned and walked away.

Molly said, "Thank you."

"Don't thank me. Just take that evil nailed choker away."

Molly called after him, "Why don't you want to go home, to your family underground?"

"Because I'm the smallest and the weakest." He kept walking as he spoke, so she barely heard the end of his answer. "And because I'm afraid of the dark…"

Molly smiled. Mr Crottel might still be afraid of the dark, but she wasn't scared of him, or his magic, or his curses, or his smelly slobbering deephound form.

She scuffed the magical boundary, and slipped the collar into her pocket. She'd return it to the cabinet at Ballindreich before the end of the holidays.

Then she started walking back towards the entrance to Stone Egg Wood. Walking slowly, trudging on her heavy human legs.

Her thoughts were moving faster than her feet. The battle had been drawing to a close when she left, but what if Corbie was now overcoming Snib, what if Mr Milne was still trying to take revenge on Innes, what if Estelle hadn't reversed all the charged-up curses? What if her friends were in danger? What if someone needed her help?

She broke into a run.

She had to find out what was happening. She had to go faster…

And she did go faster.

Molly simply remembered the fastest speed she'd ever run, and imagined shifting to her swiftest most nimble form.

And she was leaping over the heather, sprinting towards Stone Egg Wood.

Molly was a hare.

Chapter
Twenty-eight

Molly had shifted into a hare. There had been no flash of heat in her spine. She'd just shifted, gently and naturally, into her other self.

She ran across the moor, stretching out into the power and strength of her perfect sprinter's body.

When she reached the tunnel entrance, she paused, she remembered her slow heavy human legs, she imagined the best form for speaking to her friends and she walked into the tunnel as a girl.

Just inside the tunnel, she found Beth, looking out anxiously. "Molly! Are you alright?"

"I'm fine. I defeated Mr Crottel and forced him to lift the curse. I didn't use any magic spells, I just used my hare form, my girl form and that nasty collar. So I'm not cursed any more."

Beth gave her a hug. "Thank you for not becoming a witch."

"But Beth... I am still a shapeshifter. I ran back here as a hare. My curse has gone, but my shapeshifting hasn't.

I know you wanted me to lose all the magic, but I don't think I can lose the hare. I don't *want* to lose the hare."

Beth smiled. "Innes has been my friend since we were toddlers. And he's a shapeshifter, a predator, a monster and frequently very annoying, so you choosing to run as a hare occasionally won't bother me at all!"

They walked towards the wooden doors, where Innes, Theo, Atacama and Snib were waiting.

"Are you ok, Molly?" asked Innes.

She grinned. "I'm not cursed any more. But what's happening in the wood?"

Theo pushed the doors wide open.

Molly saw shattered trees, crushed nests, the earth churned up like one of Mrs Sharpe's fields, and food from the feast scattered everywhere. She also saw lots of birds and a straggling of fabled beasts, many of them limping, drooping and wrapped in bandages. But no one was fighting.

The friends moved to the side of the doorway, making space for groups of walking wounded to leave the wood.

Corbie stumbled out, followed by Mickle leading an escort of young black eagles. Corbie said to Snib, "I've resigned and I won't oppose your election as leader. But perhaps I'd be allowed to come back to the wood, once your loyal lieutenants confirm that I've returned the star iron to its original owners in the far north?"

Snib replied, "Of course, Corbie."

Theo whispered to her and she nodded. Theo waved a hand and suddenly Corbie was wearing a black cloak.

Corbie grinned, raised his arms, shifted into a glossy black crow and flew off, followed closely by the larger birds.

Snib bit her lip as she watched Corbie swoop from the tunnel into the light outside.

Then Theo touched her gently on the shoulder, and she was wearing a cloak too. "Everyone will get their wings back," he said.

Snib sighed, shifted into a crow and dived around the tunnel, somersaulting in the air. Then she landed on the ground, on her girl's feet, and said quietly, "Thanks."

As Snib tried to hide her grin and look serious, like the proper leader of a whole flock, Mr Milne limped through the doorway.

He walked right up to Innes. Molly stepped forward to defend her friend, but Beth pulled her back.

Molly saw that one side of Mr Milne's face was now smooth and unscarred, but the other was still marked with painful-looking wounds.

Mr Milne said, "Your dryad and magician friends have proved they can heal scars on my skin and scars in my memory. If your friends promise to remove all my scars, then I promise to stop hunting near our rivers. As for my revenge, Innes, I've decided that when you get home tonight, you must tell your mother – all by yourself – that you've been lying to her for months, and that you cursed your own father."

Innes turned pale. "Really? I'd almost prefer you kept hunting me..."

Mr Milne grabbed Innes's shoulders, and all the kelpie's friends moved forward to protect him.

But Mr Milne grinned, hugged his son tightly and said, "I know. That's why you're going tell her. See you at tea-time." Then he limped away.

Innes smiled, then looked at Molly. "It was easier to get him to agree to a truce once he knew I could beat him in a fight."

Mrs Sharpe walked through the doorway. "Thank you, young sphinx, for cutting me free from that woolly curse. I'll be more careful with curses and spells from now on. Maybe I should just stick to growing tatties and neeps."

"But it was your cleverly cursed chain, and the bird it trapped in the box, that allowed us to defeat Corbie," said Beth. "Please don't stop casting spells."

"Don't stop your workshops either," said Molly. "They're really useful."

"I suppose it will be safe for me to run my curse-lifting workshop in October. But I certainly won't hold any more knit-your-own-undies workshops. I never want to wear wool again."

As Mrs Sharpe strode down the tunnel, Estelle stood shining in the doorway. "Thank you all for returning me to myself. I'm embarrassed to have caused so much trouble, so before I return home, I'll use some of the extra power I foolishly stored in those mirrors to fix the stone trees." She smiled at Molly. "And thanks for tricking me into grabbing your gift. We're both much happier now."

The Keeper walked back into the wood.

"A gift!" gasped Molly. "We still don't have a birthday present for Rosalind."

"If we want to arrive at the party before she blows out her candles," said Beth, "we'd better go now."

Molly frowned, then looked round the door into the wood. "I know what we can give her!" She stepped into Stone Egg Wood. Estelle was sitting cross-legged, chatting to a small brown-black crow, as she concentrated a fraction of her energy on lifting the nearest fallen tree. By her feet was an upside-down nest.

Molly turned the nest over and found a beautiful white egg, gleaming with lines of silver light.

She picked up the egg and rejoined her friends. "The eggs won't hatch now that the crows aren't linked to curses, so we can give one to Rosalind as a toy. And I just found this gorgeous silvery egg!"

Molly, Innes, Beth, Atacama and Theo walked along the tunnel, heading for the bright winter sunlight and a birthday party. Molly stopped. "Snib, aren't you coming with us?"

"I'm not invited."

Beth said, "It's not my birthday, but the party's in my woods, so I can invite you. Come on."

And they all flew, on Theo's carpet, back to Craigvenie.

When they could see Beth's wood, Molly zipped the egg into her pocket and said, "Race you, Innes?"

"Are you sure?"

"Don't you want to know if you can win, now that I'm not cursed?"

As she leapt from the low-flying carpet, she considered racing him as a hare, but she'd won as a hare so many times. She wanted to find out what she could do now that shapeshifting was her choice not her curse.

She wondered about cheetahs and racehorses. But she decided to go back to where it all began.

Molly remembered a pursuit across playing fields, months ago, when she'd first become a hare. She remembered being chased, and then she imagined the challenge of chasing.

Molly landed on the ground as a slim sharp greyhound.

Innes landed on heavy hooves beside her.

They raced.

Molly enjoyed the smooth stride of her four equally long legs and the single-minded focus of a hunter.

She beat Innes to the edge of the woods, easily, with several paces to spare.

Then she shifted back and stood up on two human legs.

Innes laughed. "Well done, again."

The rest of them floated to the ground and Theo said, "So you've decided to claim your magic after all?"

Molly shook her head. "Shapeshifting is the only magic I plan to use. Unless," she looked round at her five friends, "unless any of you are ever in trouble, and need me to chase more complicated spells..."

Innes was still laughing.

Theo, Snib and Atacama were smiling at Molly.

But Beth was frowning.

The dryad took a deep breath, then said, "I suppose I can get used to you running about in a few other shapes and sizes..." She linked arms with Molly and led them all into the woods.

They followed the glitter of fairy lights through the shadows of the trees. When they reached the centre of the woods, Molly realised they'd been following genuine fairy lights: light balls balanced on the wands of flower fairies, who were gathered in the branches, drinking from acorn teacups.

Molly saw Rosalind in a bright red dress, Beth's aunts and uncles, and a few faces she recognised from Craigvenie, including her own Aunt Doreen, who looked a little wide-eyed. She saw Caracorum posing by a pine tree as if she was guarding it. She saw the three fungus fairies sitting quietly under a wooden table eating blue cheese sandwiches. She saw the daffodil fairy perched on a healthy rowan branch, chatting to a fairy in a primrose-yellow dress.

There were also guests Molly had never seen before, including six tumbling sphinx kittens, flying through the air on wings just big enough to carry their plump furry bodies, and a small blond boy playing conkers with Rosalind.

The birthday girl looked over and waved. "Your big brother's here, Kyle! Did you bring me a present, Innes? Did you *all* bring me a present?"

"We all went on a quest," said Molly, "we each fought

our own monsters, and we found this for you." She put the cold silver-white stone egg in Rosalind's warm hands.

Rosalind said, "Oh, it's so glittery. Thank you!"

As a ginger sphinx kitten narrowly missed Atacama's ears and crash-landed in the icing of a carrot cake, Rosalind gave the egg a sticky cuddle.

The stone egg cracked.

Rosalind gasped and dropped it.

The egg broke open, and a bird emerged from the silvery fragments.

A shining bird, with bright rainbow-coloured feathers.

The bird hopped up onto Rosalind's hand, then flew into the air. It glided elegantly round the erratic sphinxes and landed on a branch, with its long rainbow-striped tail hanging down.

Snib said, "Hello, little sister."

Rosalind said, "What a pretty present!"

Molly leant against a birch tree, her friends around her, a slice of birthday cake in her hand and a bird singing above her. A bird who'd hatched without a curse...

Molly wondered what it would be like to fly on wings of her own.

She looked through the brightly lit branches to the cloudy sky beyond, and she smiled.

Perhaps she'd find out tomorrow.

Also by Lari Don

FABLED BEAST CHRONICLES

It's not every day a grumpy, injured centaur appears on your doorstep. And that's just the beginning...

Helen's first aid kit comes in very handy when she meets Yann's friends – a fairy, a dragon, a phoenix, a werewolf and even a selkie – who have a habit of getting into trouble.

Together they must solve riddles, fight fauns and defeat the dangerous Master of the Maze before midwinter and the end of the world.

"A gripping fairytale that will keep you reading past your bedtime." Cait, age 8

Including
First Aid for Fairies and Other Fabled Beasts
WINNER OF A SCOTTISH CHILDREN'S BOOK AWARD

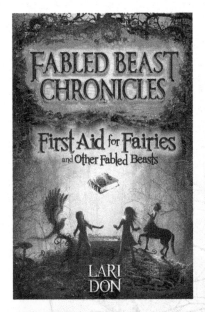

FABLED BEAST CHRONICLES

First Aid for Fairies
and Other Fabled Beasts

LARI DON

FABLED BEAST CHRONICLES

Wolf Notes
and
Other Musical Mishaps

LARI DON

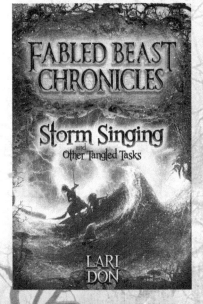

FABLED BEAST CHRONICLES

Storm Singing
and
Other Tangled Tasks

LARI DON

FABLED BEAST CHRONICLES

Maze Running
and
Other Magical Missions

LARI DON

Discover the story behind Molly's curse

Molly hesitated. "Are you cursed?"

The girl nodded. "Aren't you?"

Curses aren't real. So Molly Drummond definitely can't be magically cursed. Can she?

When Molly finds herself in a curse-lifting workshop with four magical classmates – a kelpie, a dryad, a sphinx and a toad – she's determined not to believe in it. But it's true that whenever a dog barks, Molly suddenly becomes a small and very fast hare…

Now she's friends with a whole team of magical creatures all searching for a way to free her from her curse.

Follow Molly into a world of brilliant magic, unexpected adventure and extraordinary friendship in the first two books of Lari Don's breathtaking *Spellchasers* trilogy.

ᑌᛃ🐾ᛏᛉ

"Exciting, thrilling and breathtaking." Emily, age 9

"Absolutely brilliant." Isabel, age 9

"What more could you want from a book?" Tomasz, age 11

"An exciting fantasy quest." Lucy, age 8

EMBRACE THE MAGIC.
DEFY DESTINY.

One sunny morning the triplets disappear,
leaving only a few mysterious clues behind.

Older sister Pearl sets out to find them. Her journey
unfolds into an incredible and perilous adventure.

Can Pearl save her brother and sisters
from the unknown fate that lies ahead?